Christie
&Company

Christie &Company

KATHERINE HALL PAGE

AVON BOOKS NEW YORK

CHRISTIE & COMPANY is an original publication of Avon Books. This work has never before appeared in book form. This work is a novel. Any similarity to actual persons or events is purely coincidental.

AVON BOOKS
A division of
The Hearst Corporation
1350 Avenue of the Americas
New York, New York 10019

Copyright © 1996 by Katherine Hall Page
Map by Virginia Norey
Published by arrangement with the author
Library of Congress Catalog Card Number: 96-20016
ISBN: 0-380-97393-6
RL: 5.0

Library of Congress Cataloging in Publication Data:

Page, Katherine Hall.
    Christie & Company / Katherine Hall Page.—1st ed.
        p.   cm.
Summary: Three new eighth-grade girls at Cabot School find that their shared interest in mysteries comes in handy when the roommates are blamed for a series of thefts at the school.
[1. Mystery and detective stories.   2. Boarding schools—Fiction.   3. Schools—Fiction.]   I. Title.
PZ7.P142Ch   1996   96-20016
[Fic]—dc20   CIP

First Avon Books Hardcover Printing: October 1996

AVON TRADEMARK REG. U.S. PAT. OFF. AND IN OTHER COUNTRIES, MARCA REGISTRADA, HECHO EN U.S.A.

Printed in the U.S.A.

FIRST EDITION

QPM   10   9   8   7   6   5   4   3   2   1

For my son, Nicholas,
who wanted me to write a book he could read

Acknowledgments

I would like to thank the Thompson Island Outward Bound Education Center in Boston for all their help and a wonderful day.

Also Lisa Bergmann, Carolyn Grunst, Emily Traverse, for letting me eavesdrop, and Anne Struble, for all the diving information.

"It has this advantage," said Poirot. "If you confront anyone who has lied with the truth, they usually admit it—often out of sheer surprise. It is only necessary to guess *right* to produce your effect."

—Agatha Christie, *Murder on the Orient Express*

Maintenance bldgs.

New Dorms

Foreign languages

Faculty Housing

Faculty Housing

Classrooms/ Humanities

Pond

Cabot/Mansfield Riding Center

Dorm

Paths/ hills

Classrooms (Science bldg.)

← To Aleford Center

Main Road

Art/drama/ music bldg.

Main Entrance →

The Cabot School
Aleford, Massachusetts

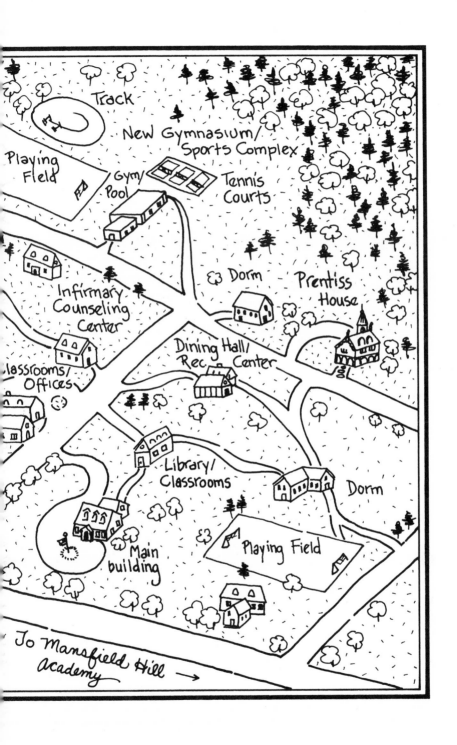

❖Chapter One

CHRISTIE MONTGOMERY SAT UP STRAIGHT in the passenger seat of her father's car. Her spine barely grazed the leather seat cover of his new Lexus. The windows were closed. She couldn't hear the traffic that swirled about them. Inside the cocoon the car made, there was total silence.

"Mind if I turn on the radio?"

"No, go ahead."

Christie started pushing buttons randomly, country-western blaring out for a millisecond, then Pearl Jam giving way in turn to some whining, confessional talk show.

"Try WGBH, number three."

She pushed the button and something classical by someone she probably should know ended the search. It was noise, anyway.

"Sibelius. One of your mother's favorites."

Christie nodded and tried to listen more attentively, but the combination of her father's casual mention of her mother and the fact that at the end of this drive was a new school made any serious music appreciation impossible. How could he mention Mom like that? So, well, so casually—as if she were off shopping at the Chestnut Hill Mall or gone for the weekend to visit her parents in Connecticut? How could he mention her as if she were coming back and would listen to this music by Sibelwhoever, when she would never hear any music by anybody again?

Christie had passed beyond the stage where she cried whenever she thought of her mother. Now there was just a slightly sick feeling and her stomach knotted up. During really bad times, she felt as if she was going to faint. It wasn't something she talked about with her father. Not that he didn't want to. Just last night, he'd knocked on her bedroom door while she was finishing her packing, then came in and sat on the edge of her bed.

"Are you all right with this going away to school thing? I hate to do it, but I'll be traveling even more this year than last. Hallie has been terrific, but I can't ask her to stay full-time any longer. I know she misses her own place." Hallie, Mrs. Halliday, had worked for Christie's mother's family and when Molly Montgomery developed cancer, Hallie had moved in, staying to the end and then some.

"Cabot will be fine, Dad. They have a great pool and the coach seemed really nice." Christie had been diving competitively for years. When she'd gone to visit the campus, the first person she'd asked to meet was the swim coach.

"You'll be able to come home a lot of weekends and, of course, during the holidays."

The impulse to make her father feel even more guilty

passed. For the space of a moment, she'd felt sorry for him.

"Really, it's going to work out great. I'm sure I'll make lots of friends and be elected Miss Cabot or something."

He'd laughed at that and reached out to hug her. She tried not to stiffen, but from the look on his face, she knew he felt it.

"She's gone, honey. We can't bring her back. I wish to God we could. We only have each other. It's just you and me, kid," he'd whispered into her blond hair, cut short for diving.

Now in the car, she ran her fingers across her part, lifting the silken fringe that fell across her cheek back into place for an instant. Just you and me. She matched her footsteps to the words as she got out of the car and walked across the parking lot to Prentiss House, the dorm she'd been assigned.

"Christie, shouldn't we take your things in?"

She'd totally forgotten about the footlocker, assorted sports equipment, and other luggage crowded in the backseat and the trunk of the car.

"Let's find my room first, okay?"

"Sure."

Her father's long stride caught up to her easily. Calvin Montgomery was in his mid-thirties, but he still looked boyish—a look that often fooled the other side in court. A cowlick that tended to sprout up as he was approaching the bench and jackets missing buttons, even when Christie's mom was alive, had falsely reassured those colleagues not familiar with his reputation, a reputation earned by countless hours away from home—hours he might now regret but could not regain.

3

Father and daughter stood for a moment gazing up at Prentiss House, the eighth-grade dorm for boarders and gathering place for eighth-grade day students. It was a large Victorian house, resplendent with gingerbread trim on the roof and gables, a deep front porch, a turret, and, to crown the cake, an incongruous, decorative widow's walk, completely nonfunctional, as the Cabot School was many miles inland. No captain's wife had ever searched the horizon for the sign of a sail. Even if they had been close to shore, the size of the walk would have made any pacing on her part as treacherous as her husband's voyage.

"What a place!" Cal Montgomery laughed. "Well, it's got plenty of atmosphere. Let's hope the mattresses are a bit more up-to-date."

There was no one in the living room, reassuringly furnished in comfortable-looking chairs and a large couch. Christie spotted a list of names next to the fire-drill instructions on the bulletin board in the hall and discovered her room number was thirteen. Its connection to bad luck crossed her mind. She supposed boarding schools weren't like hotels, skipping thirteenth floors and room number thirteens altogether.

"Thirteen must be upstairs," Christie said.

"Where is everybody? I don't like it that there isn't anybody here to meet you. Where's the housemother?" Her father was annoyed.

At the bottom of the staircase, they heard voices coming from the end of the hall and followed the sound. Three girls were in a large room with the door open. Their laughter stopped when they saw Christie and her father in the doorway.

4

"We're looking for the housemother," Cal said, "and room thirteen."

Was it Christie's imagination or did the three exchange glances?

"Terry—that's the housemother—had to go to the main office to get some forms or something. She'll be right back. Room thirteen is up two flights. Turn left. The number's on the door."

The girl who answered hadn't changed her position. She was slouched comfortably on the bolsters of a studio couch that Christie assumed must be a bed. She had long, thick blond hair and big blue eyes, and she was wearing jeans and a black T-shirt. Perversely, Christie was glad to note the tiniest of zits just starting to erupt at the corner of this beauty's mouth. The girl at her side looked like a younger version and was probably her sister. The third girl had stood up when they entered and seemed to have some manners.

"Welcome to Cabot. I'm Elaine Feld. Also known as 'Ellie,' except when you say it fast with Feld, it sounds like Babar's cousin. Meet Marcia and Jessica Lloyd. We're letting Jess in today as a special treat. She's a lowly sixth grader."

"I'm Christie Montgomery, and this is my father. It's nice to meet you all. See you later." Christie didn't feel like sticking around and was pretty sure the feeling was mutual—at least on the part of the two sisters, who had still made only slight nods of acknowledgment as gestures of welcome.

"Good-bye, ladies. Time to track down room thirteen—and the elusive housemother." Her father's charm brought some giggles, and Christie was glad to be in the corridor again.

"What kind of housemother is called Terry?" Cal wondered. "Aren't they all supposed to be Mrs. Somebody, elderly but spry and very responsible?"

"I'm sure whoever she is, she's responsible, Dad. They wouldn't hire a ditz."

Room thirteen turned out to include the turret, much to Christie's delight, had high ceilings and a large casement window with a window seat tucked beneath. It was at the rear of the house, overlooking a small parking area, garage, and woods beyond. The moldings and plaster floral garlands that encircled several wall sconces were all the decorative touches that remained from the original house. The rest of the room was "Dorm Modern"—plain, sturdy-looking wooden furniture and industrial carpeting somewhere between brown and gray. There were two studio couches, desks, chairs, and dressers in the main room, then one of each in the smaller turret off to the side. It didn't have a door, but it was still very private—almost like having a single, which unfortunately, she'd learned, were only in the dorms for upperclasswomen. She took off her jacket and laid it decisively on the bed, staking her claim.

"Let's get my stuff. I'd like to get unpacked, then go do some laps."

"Are you sure you want to be off by yourself? Maybe you should wait until the other girls come."

"I'm sure, Dad." And she was.

Cal Montgomery had a plane to catch. After helping Christie lug her things up to her room, he kissed her good-bye and went to the main building in search of the housemother and Mrs. Babcox, Cabot's headmistress.

It didn't take Christie long to put her things away. Her wardrobe, courtesy of the Gap and Express, had been planned mainly for ease and comfort. The fact that she looked great—her slender, long-legged swimmer's body, hair blonder than usual from the summer sun, and blue eyes that looked green in some lights—didn't really occur to her.

The pool was open and she slipped into the water with a sigh of relief. Her home, her refuge. When her face was already wet, no one could tell whether there were tears or not. Sometimes she wasn't sure herself. She set off down the lap lane at a furious rate. Just you and me. Just you and me. If it had had to be only two of them, why hadn't it been Mom? And how did you live with that thought—that you wished your father dead? She tasted salt in her mouth instead of chlorine and swam faster.

Maggie Porter peered into the thick early-morning Maine fog. The ferry landing had completely disappeared and her parents and younger brother, Willy, were disembodied voices—their last, lingering good-byes echoing across the cove. Soon these stopped and she heard the car start up, stall as usual, then take off.

She was on her own.

Her hand went to her mouth in a swift, practiced motion and she was about to nibble a nail when she abruptly thrust the offending fingers into her jeans pocket. She was not, repeat *not,* going to continue biting her nails at boarding school. The girls in the pictures in the Cabot School catalog—sitting in their dorm rooms, playing sports, studying—hadn't looked like nail-biters. They hadn't looked nervous at all. Maggie sighed and stared over the side of the boat at where she knew the water to be, the sound of the waves oddly reassuring as the boat steadily plied its familiar course between Little Bittern Island and the mainland. Not being able to see much of anything heightened her other senses—the cries of the gulls sounded more raucous than usual and more distinct. She even thought she could detect a faint smell of pine above the paint and fuel smells of the ferry. She breathed deeply and tasted the salt spray in the air.

There were only a few other passengers on board and they were all inside. Maggie had wanted to be alone. She was tired of answering the question, "How do you think you're going to like going to school up to Massachusetts?" (Little Bittern was, of course, Down East.) She varied her replies from noncommittal to guarded enthusiasm. In truth, it was an answer she wanted to find herself.

The fog didn't seem to be lifting much, but Maggie knew that in an hour or so it would burn off, revealing another perfect sunny Maine day—blue skies filled with the big puffy white clouds she and Willy liked to imagine into everything from Beavis and Butt-head (Willy's contribution) to fairy-tale castles. They'd had a string of these days since late August and it had made the prospect of leaving just that much more confusing.

Maggie pushed her hands into the opposite sleeves of her sweatshirt and gripped her wrists. It was cool up on deck in the fog. The fog. She leaned against the rail and rested her chin on her swaddled arms.

"Only you can find your way in this cursed pea souper, Margaret. We know you won't let us down." His voice was confident as he locked the burnished leather attaché case containing the secret documents onto her slender wrist. His touch was light, but lingering. "I'll be waiting for your return." She turned up

8

the collar of her Burberry trench coat and prepared to move off into the night. He stopped her, placing a hand on each shoulder and looking deeply into her brown eyes, brown eyes with tiny flecks of gold, and said, "Margaret, I can't keep it to myself any longer. I must tell you—"

"So, how do you think you're going to like going to school up to Massachusetts? I went to Boston once. Didn't care for it much. Too many people. Too much traffic."

Maggie spun around. It was Cliff Compton. He ran the only garage on Little Bittern.

"The school's not actually in Boston," Maggie replied. "It's in Aleford, west of the city. It's more like the country there." Her mother had graduated from Cabot, and any mention of Aleford was apt to bring a slight mistiness to her eyes, plus endless reminiscences of all the outdoorsy fun she'd had in her years at the school—hikes through the woods during fall foliage season, cross-country skiing, berry picking, mayflowers. Maggie was a little surprised that her mother's enthusiasm hadn't killed any desire on Maggie's part to go to Cabot. The normal order of things was to hate what Mom liked and like what Mom hated, at least where clothes, music, and friends were concerned. But Maggie *did* want to go to Cabot. She knew there would be times when she'd long for home, but taking the ferry back and forth to school every day with the handful of other island kids in junior and senior high last year had been a drag.

The Porters had come to Little Bittern from New York City four years ago, when Maggie was nine, to restore and open the Blue Heron Inn, which was just beginning to show a profit. The whole family had pitched in, scraping layers of old wallpaper from the walls, replacing worn shingles, painting the wicker rockers on the long front porch, and helping Julia Porter test new recipes. Somehow, they had gotten through the first summer and things had become easier as they learned some of the tricks of the trade. Julia Porter had been famous for her dinner parties back in the city, but it was another thing to turn out interesting fare for an innful of people night after night. She'd cut out some of the pricey, complicated gourmet dishes, replacing them with others—just as delicious, her family thought—based on local supplies and the inn's own garden.

The payback for all their work was long months together when the inn closed in the off-season. The island's elementary school had been fine, but Maggie knew she was learning more than other kids from her father's astronomy lessons, her mother's informal art-history tutoring—complete with sessions where they tried to paint or carve like the artists—and reading aloud in front of the fire each night, often while a winter storm raged outside. When she went to school on the mainland, she was so tired by the time she got home, all she wanted to do was grab something to eat and roll into bed. Because of the ferry schedule, the island kids stayed on at school, doing their homework and participating in after-school activities. When she did sit by the fire at home, she promptly nodded off.

By the middle of the year, the Porters realized that they weren't seeing much of Maggie during the week and Maggie admitted that some of her classes weren't very challenging. Boarding school seemed to make sense. A few of Maggie's friends weren't too happy at school, either, and she felt a little guilty that she had the chance to change her life merely because her mother was an alum of a place that offered special scholarships to its graduates' daughters.

It was still foggy. She could hear the bell on one of the channel markers tolling eerily in the still morning air. Cliff had gone in after their brief interchange and Maggie suddenly decided to follow him. She wanted to see people talking, drinking coffee—normal stuff. Out here, there was too much fog. Fog hid things, and Maggie wasn't sure she wanted to know what was there. She could hear her mother saying, Miss Overactive Imagination. Maybe it was true; she *was* having trouble shaking off a strong feeling of dread—a feeling enveloping her like the fog. It wasn't homesickness—at least not yet. No, this was more like that old saying some of the islanders had when they got the creeps: "Someone's walking across your grave." Well, someone was definitely walking across hers, Maggie thought.

"Vicky! Victoria! This is the last time I'm calling you! We're late! You know your father and I don't have much time!"

"Don't worry, Mom. I'll be down in a sec." Thirteen-year-old Vicky Lee took one last appraising look at herself in the full-length mirror on the back of her closet door. Satisfied with what she saw there, she left her bedroom without a backward glance and ran to the living room, where her parents and grandmother were waiting. The image the mirror had reflected would have pleased most girls her age—long, gleaming, straight black hair, smooth ivory skin, dark almond-shaped eyes below brows that seemed to have been painted by nature in a position of delighted surprise. She was wearing a short, pleated plaid skirt, an over-sized white oxford-cloth shirt, one of her father's striped ties, and a cropped black velvet jacket she'd been thrilled to find in a secondhand store in Cambridge. It was her "schoolgirl" look for the first day of school and she was sure she wouldn't see anyone else wearing what she was. Vicky had every intention of standing out at Cabot and figured she might as well start on Day One.

"Oh no! Not another suitcase," her father wailed in only partially mock despair.

"It's small. I'll hold it on my lap. Don't worry."

"My little peacock," her grandmother said indulgently.

Vicky's mother was less forgiving. "You can come home and get anything you need. You're packing as if you were going around the world."

Vicky just smiled. An only child, she had learned early on that if she kept quiet and didn't try to fight back, she'd usually get what she wanted. Lately, she'd added the phrase "Don't worry," and the remark had become so ubiquitous that her parents, especially her father, tended to laugh when she said it—forgetting even more what they wanted or didn't want her to do.

"Isn't that my tie?" Her father reached for the bright silk.

Vicky pulled away. "Daddy! Don't mess me up. I'm only borrowing it. Please?"

"I don't understand these fashions. At least tuck in your shirt. That's not one of mine, too, is it?"

"No, it's mine," Vicky said, making no move to change what had been so artfully constructed.

"Well, what are we waiting for," Mr. Lee said. "This is a big day. Our daughter is leaving home."

"But not for long. And not far. I'll be back every weekend I can."

The adults nodded. They wanted the best for Vicky and had selected Cabot after looking at many schools, but without her, it would be dull around the apartment and at the restaurant they owned.

Henry and Virginia Lee had come to the United States from Hong Kong when Vicky was a baby. Henry Lee had been an accountant there. Virginia had worked in a dress shop. With their savings and that of Henry's mother, they had been able to open a tiny take-out restaurant in Brookline, Massachusetts. It had expanded into the adjoining stores to become the Ginger Jar, one of the area's most popular Chinese restaurants.

Early last Sunday morning, there had been a gathering at the restaurant of all Vicky's numerous aunts, uncles, and cousins to say good-bye and good luck. Outgoing Vicky was a favorite and beloved member of the family. It had been a great party—and great food. They had consumed trayfuls of dim sum, little dishes of stuffed dumplings, shrimp balls, spareribs, and other delicacies. Now Vicky felt a hunger pang as she stood close to her grandmother in the elevator taking them down to the parking garage. She had no illusions about the kind of food she'd be getting at Cabot. If there was anything resembling the Cantonese cuisine she'd known since birth, it would be chow mein—or American chop suey, a truly weird dish that had turned up occasionally for lunch at her elementary school—ground beef, macaroni, and cooked celery. Ugh! She laughed out loud.

"What's so funny?" her father asked.

"I'm going to miss you, but I think I may miss the Ginger Jar more."

"Thank you very much," Henry Lee said as he opened the door for his mother and helped settle her in. Even though the September day was mild, she was wearing a quilted silk jacket he'd bought her on his last trip to Hong Kong to find a new chef. Every time he hugged his mother, she seemed thinner and her bones more fragile. He pushed the thought from his mind and concentrated on the happiness of this day.

"Everyone set?" He started the car, only a year old, and drove out into the street, conscious of the pride he felt at having provided so well for his family.

"I hope there will be at least one other Chinese girl. If you don't have anyone to talk to, you'll forgot how to speak," old Mrs. Lee fretted.

"Don't worry, Grandmother." This time, Vicky added more words. "I'll be calling you so much, you'll be sick of the sound of my voice."

Her father turned on the radio to listen to the weather. Rain meant more customers on the weekend, as people tended to stay in town, then got restless and wanted to eat out—or in with a video. Either way meant business.

Virginia Lee had been quiet since they left the apartment, and Vicky wondered what her mother was thinking. It was something she wondered a lot. Vicky, never shy with others, found it almost impossible to communicate with her mother. She tried to remember when she had stopped feeling free to say anything, when that feeling of being held at arm's length had started. A year ago? Two years ago? She knew her mother loved her. It was in her eyes. But a shade dropped down over those same eyes whenever Vicky tried to talk about anything personal. "I have to work now," was her mother's invariable excuse, and in fact it was true most of the time. Both parents put in long hours at the restaurant and their inability to be at home with Vicky was one of the reasons they had considered boarding school in the first place. Henry's mother lived with them and had taken care of Vicky since she was born, but she could not be expected to manage a teenager—especially a headstrong, exuberant one like Vicky.

She was wriggling in her seat now, impatient to get to Aleford. An all-girl school in the sticks! Was she crazy? Mansfield Hill Academy, all boys, was someplace in Aleford, too. She'd read in the catalog that they shared some activities—plays, ski trips, clubs like the astronomy club—Mansfield had an observatory. Big deal! She vowed to find some excitement or die trying.

She breathed on the glass window and wrote her initials, looking through the *V L* at the other cars on the turnpike. She wondered what her roommates would be like. Her "Welcome to Cabot" letter had said there were two of them: Margaret Porter and Christie Montgomery. One thing was certain: Neither girl would speak Chinese.

The ferry hit the pier with a resounding thud. Mrs. Moses, who was driving down to Boston to see her sister and had offered to give Maggie a ride, was waving cheerfully from the dock. A five-hour drive. Maybe Maggie could fall asleep, or pretend to. Conscious or unconscious, she'd be at Cabot by suppertime, or maybe they called it dinner. Her roommates would be there long before she would. She hoped they'd like her. Of course they will. What's not to like? She heard her mother's voice in her ears as she watched them unload the cars before the passengers could get off. She heard her own answer, too: a homely girl from the boonies, never mind those years in New York City, with glasses, too curly, long, mousey brown hair, and a tendency to space out.

"Yoo hoo! Maggie! Are you excited?" called Mrs. Moses.

Strangely enough, Maggie was.

❖Chapter Two

THE TRIP TO ALEFORD HAD TAKEN EVEN longer than Maggie had predicted. Mrs. Moses was definitely a candidate for an I BRAKE FOR FACTORY OUT-LETS bumper sticker. Maggie had heard her say, ''You don't mind, dear, just a quick look'' so often, she'd finally gone to sleep in self-defense. When they got to Aleford, it was obviously too late for the evening meal and Mrs. Moses had insisted they go to a ''nice'' restaurant to make amends. All Maggie had wanted was to grab a Big Mac and get to Cabot. She was dreading being the last to arrive and had sacrificed a thumbnail to her nervousness.

Dinner had seemed interminable. Maggie quickly said she couldn't eat another bite when the waitress asked them if they wanted dessert, then had had to sit and watch Mrs. Moses consume a delectable-looking piece of German chocolate cake. It was past seven o'clock when they pulled up in front of Prentiss House, after getting lost and circling around the campus several times.

They said good-bye to each other with what Maggie

was sure was mutual relief. Mrs. Moses did manage to whisper, "Your housemother looks a little young" on her way out, but at that point Maggie would have settled for one of the Muppet Babies in residence.

Theresa McNeill—"Call me Terry; everyone does"—did look young—younger even than her twenty-five years. She was wearing a long flowered dress, Doc Martens, and her shoulder-length light brown hair was pulled back into a wispy ponytail with a bright purple scrunch.

She had greeted Maggie warmly. "Follow me. I know you must be anxious to see your room. You'll like your roommates. They're new, too. Eighth graders are allowed to choose their own roommies, which usually leaves the new girls together, unless they already know somebody here. But it doesn't take long for everybody to be one happy family. I went to Cabot myself, so you can take it as gospel."

Maggie felt extremely tired, and the bag she was lugging seemed filled with lead instead of clothes. Her footlocker had been shipped on ahead and she fervently hoped it had arrived.

It was sitting in the middle of the floor when they opened the door, and she felt better than she had for hours. Terry made hasty introductions, told them there would be an all-house meeting in the living room at eight, followed by cocoa and cookies, then left to do "a gazillion and one things."

Christie came out of her alcove to greet the new arrival, a book in hand, finger marking the place, which indicated a desire to get back to her reading as quickly as possible. The three looked at one another awkwardly until Vicky said, "Do you want help unpacking? You get this dresser and half the closet."

"That's okay. I'll do it myself." This sounded rude, so Maggie added, "I mean, I should probably do it myself; then I'll know where everything is." The problem with being shy was that you could come off as just the opposite—some kind of stuck-up egomaniac who could care less what other people thought. In fact, Maggie cared a little too much.

"Whatever," Vicky said, and sat down on her bed. Christie stood uncertainly by Maggie's trunk.

"I put the key in a really safe place and now I can't find it, of course," Maggie said, digging frantically through her open suitcase, disturbing the neat packing job she and her mother had done, and exposing for all to see what she now thought of, after one look at Vicky, as terminally boring clothes. "I hate when this happens."

The room was quiet again, but not for long.

"Look, you two," Vicky burst out, "I'm a talker and a doer. I can't shut up for long or sit still. I like to call it energy. My friends sometimes call it other things— *bossy* being one of the kinder words—so feel free to object. My feelings can't be hurt—at least not this way. So, let me help you find your key and then I'll hand you your stuff and you can put it where you want."

While Vicky had been talking, Maggie had continued to search. Now she held up the key triumphantly. "In my sneaker toe. One job accomplished." Reversing her earlier decision, she told Vicky gratefully, "I'd be happy for your help with the rest."

Christie had still not said anything.

"What are you reading?" Vicky asked. The girl looked so uncomfortable. Maybe she was homesick.

"Nothing, just a mystery."

"Just a mystery!" Maggie shot back, "I love mysteries and read them all the time. I wish we could read mysteries instead of half the dumb things my English teachers have made me read."

Vicky nodded. "I love mysteries, too. Last year, I was lucky. My teacher let me do a project on them, starting with *The Moonstone*. That was really the first detective mystery."

Christie offered her first unsolicited remark. "Yeah, Wilkie Collins. It was great. I couldn't stop reading it."

"Three mystery nuts! Do you think that's why they put us together? I did list it first under "interests" on the application form," Maggie wondered.

"Me, too, but that's not why we're together. It's because we're the only new eighth graders this year and all the old girls wanted to room with each other," Vicky told them.

"Terry said I'd be rooming with two other new girls, but not that we were the only new kids in the whole class," Maggie said. She had been a new girl—and an off-islander—when they'd moved to Maine, and last year she'd been new again—and an islander—when she'd started school on the mainland. She'd never met an adult who'd really understood the significance of these categories and how being in one made you feel—especially not her parents.

Again, Christie didn't say anything, but Vicky immediately sympathized. "Yeah, it's a drag. You *know* the cliques have probably been in place for years—especially if they've been here since the beginning."

Cabot girls started boarding in the seventh grade, but there was a lower school for day students. It was smaller and began with the fourth grade. The older Cabot students called the younger girls the "Caboteers."

Vicky continued to explain. "Ninth grade is when most new kids come and things may get shaken up then. There aren't even any new eighth-grade day students. We are the only new kids in 'Widow.' "

"Widow?" Christie sounded puzzled.

"That's the nickname for Prentiss House—because of that widow's walk on the roof." Vicky had picked up a lot of information during the afternoon. She'd been hanging out at the student center while Christie did laps and Maggie watched Mrs. Moses buy panty hose for the year.

" 'Black Widow' is more like it," Maggie said dismally, thinking of the way the house had looked when she'd arrived—silhouetted against the evening sky, dark clouds hovering over the sharp points of the elaborate Victorian trim.

The moist heat clung to the vines surrounding the campsite the team had hastily set up. They were too weary to continue their search for the missing scientist and his beautiful young daughter. Dark fell as suddenly as a closing night curtain. A bird screeched from deep within the jungle. Philip Vanderheusen stretched out on the ground, close to the fire they'd made to keep the animals away. A moment later, he leaped to his feet, knife drawn, as something came crashing through the underbrush. It was the doctor, and he was carrying the lifeless form of his daughter in his arms! "Black Widow!" he cried hoarsely, "She was bitten on the leg while helping me reach a specimen. Damn this orchid collection!" Philip quickly reached for the young woman. "I can suck the venom out. There may still be time!"

"Earth to Maggie! Where are you?"

Both Christie and Vicky were looking at her with quizzical expressions on their faces. Maggie realized she was holding one ski sock, having intended to search for the other before she got distracted.

She blushed. "I have a tendency to daydream."

"I guess." Christie laughed. "You were really gone. I wish I could disappear like that." She sounded genuinely envious.

"I think I'm a little nervous, too," Maggie admitted.

Vicky slung her arm around Maggie's shoulders. "Don't worry. Three is better than one, and maybe there will be some more mystery lovers. Which reminds me— what are you reading, anyway, Christie? Don't tell me it's an Agatha Christie."

Christie shook her head and smiled for the first time. "It's a new one by Joan Lowery Nixon, but I do like to read Agatha Christie. I was named for her."

"Wow, your parents must be into mysteries big-time," Vicky enthused.

"It's because of how they met. They were both reading Agatha Christie's *Death on the Nile* while sitting across from each other on the subway."

It was a story Christie had heard so many times, she could recite it by heart. As a little girl, she used to beg her mother to tell it to her "just one more time" before she went to sleep at night. They called it "The True Story of How Christie Montgomery Got Her Name."

"That's so romantic," Maggie said, taking a pile of

sweatshirts from Vicky's hands and putting them in the dresser drawer.

"Good thing they went for Christie instead of Agatha," Vicky commented. "Or what if they had both been reading Rex Stout?"

Maggie and Christie both laughed.

"I don't know which would have been worse, Rex or Stout. Do you have brothers or sisters with mysterious names, too?" Maggie asked.

Christie's face clouded over. It was a dramatic change. "No, I'm the only one."

"Like me," Vicky said, "an adored, slightly spoiled only child. Life could be worse."

But Christie scarcely heard her new roommate's words. Her parents had wanted another child, maybe even more than one, but first nothing happened. Then her mother's cancer was diagnosed and all thoughts of children ended. All thoughts of everything ended. She wondered what it would have been like to have had a sibling, someone to share what she had gone through. The raised hopes, the deep despair when they were dashed, and then that final dark valley. To share what she was going through now.

Vicky's persistent voice broke into Christie's thoughts. "Are you okay? Hello. It's almost cocoa and cookies time."

"I'm fine. On into the lion's den." Christie attempted to keep her voice light.

What is the matter with this girl? Vicky thought. Her reverie had been distinctly different from Maggie's. Christie seemed to be retreating into a place she didn't want to go, while from the expression on daydreamer Maggie's face, her imagination was a cherished retreat.

At least Christie had laughed a few times this evening, which was more than she'd done at dinner. She'd arrived at the room just minutes before, her hair still wet from the pool. Vicky was brushing her hair, and after introductions, she told Christie she had better hurry up and dry hers so they wouldn't be late. Christie had replied that it just dried itself, and the two girls went off. Vicky believed that nature could always be helped by art, but she was impressed when Christie's short hair quickly dried out in a sleek cap of shiny waves.

As they started down the stairs, Maggie asked Christie, "Are your parents still big mystery fans?" eliciting the answer to Vicky's earlier thought.

Christie turned around, stopped, and faced them. "My Dad probably hasn't picked up anything except a legal brief since that subway ride, and my mother died of cancer last year."

It felt like a stab wound. Maggie breathed in sharply. "I'm so sorry—"

Christie cut her off. "Let's get going. It's bad enough to be new without being the last ones there."

Terry McNeill had exchanged her boots for slippers in the shape of mallard ducks. She sat in a big wing chair facing the girls. The contrast between her slippers and what she was saying was threatening to give Maggie the giggles, and once she started, it was hard to stop.

"I think you are all old enough to behave like responsible members of our community without my having to make a list of a gazillion rules."

"Gazillion" seemed to be Terry's favorite number, Maggie thought, and felt the laughter in the back of her throat pushing against her lips. She gave a little cough and pulled herself together. Nerves, she told herself, nothing but nerves. She glanced at her roommates. They seemed to be closing their mouths with particular force and their eyes were dancing also. Something else they had in common? Maggie sometimes laughed so hard with her friends that she was forced to race for the bathroom. "From whence," her friend Charlene in Maine had said at one of those times, "cometh the rude expression, I laughed so hard I nearly peed my pants." Her combination of the sacred—they were reading *Romeo and Juliet* in school at the time—and the profane had set them all off again. Maggie looked nervously around the Prentiss House living room, checking the exits.

It was a pretty room, done in shades of rose and deep blue, with heavy ivory drapes at the long windows overlooking the beautifully landscaped campus. The carpet was a richly patterned Oriental. A large fireplace at one end of the room held logs for the cold winter nights that would arrive before anyone was ready. A bookcase stood to one side of the door to the hall. It contained an encyclopedia, various other reference works, and a wide range of fiction and nonfiction. Maggie spied a collection of Ngaio Marsh mysteries and took it as a good sign.

Terry was reminding the girls to sign up for the house jobs and that room inspection would be on random days.

"Remember, it wasn't that long ago that I was here, too, and I know how we'd all race around cleaning up on Thursdays. I'm not a neatness freak, but in an old house like this, you have to keep your wastebaskets emptied, use irons only in the common room on each floor, and absolutely no hot plates or anything like that. We don't want to go up in a puff of smoke.

"And try to keep food in the rooms to a minimum."

The three new girls looked puzzled.

"Ants," she explained. "Gracious living in a house like this requires some sacrifices. Next year, when you're in the brand-new ninth-grade dorm, you'll miss this funky old place.

"Now, do I have to go into all the other stuff in the handbook or can I assume you won't do anything stupid? No guys in your rooms, no going into town without permission. . . ." The girls groaned. "And above all, this is majorly important, do not, I repeat, do not affix anything to your newly painted walls except with the gummy adhesive that will peel off again. You can get that at Daniel's Hardware on Main Street."

Christie stopped listening. She'd read the handbook. She could live with the rules. All that mattered to her was that she got enough practice time. She looked about. There were twenty-four girls in the room and the expressions on their faces ranged from somewhat attentive to outright bored. Marcia Lloyd, the girl she'd met earlier, didn't attempt to disguise her feelings—she was yawning and talking to the girl next to her. The largest group was gathered around the couch, sitting on it, leaning up against it. Marcia was squarely in the middle. She'd added a flannel shirt over her T-shirt. It was nothing special, except it did sport a little Ralph Lauren horse. Cabot was noted for its riding program, and Christie wondered whether the logo represented a commitment to that or to expensive brands.

"Now it's time for volunteers," Terry said brightly. There were more groans. "Now, now, no cocoa and cookies until all these sheets are filled.'' She shook her finger mockingly and a few girls laughed.

"A fate worse than death.'' Marcia pretended to swoon. "What's up? The picnic?''

Christie was surprised to see Marcia leap to volunteer, but then, maybe she liked to be in charge.

"We can start with the picnic. It's the parent-student picnic on Sunday. It gives everyone a chance to get acquainted,'' she added for the new girls' benefit. "I need greeters, servers, and cleaner-uppers.''

Her sheets were quickly filled. Maggie figured she'd be a server and keep busy, since there was no way her parents could come. Vicky decided to be a greeter. Her parents were coming and she wanted to be free to steer them around during the event. Christie signed up to serve, too. She'd keep Maggie company. Her dad had said he would try to turn up, but Christie had heard that before.

"Now, on to the house jobs. The election for class officers and Cabot Council class reps will have to wait for the first eighth-grade meeting, which I believe is Tuesday. We'll be talking about the eighth-grade over-night then, too. This year, we're going to an Outward Bound program on Cape Cod. And yes, the boys from Mansfield Hill will be coming, too.'' There were a few cheers, and Terry gazed around the room, pretending to look severe. "Our tents will be on opposite sides of the pond, of course.'' When her glance took in the new girls, she explained further. "Each class, day students and boarders, goes on a campout someplace the first weekend of the school year. Bonding, all that good stuff, and also because if we do it any later, you'd end up freezing to death.''

Terry was beaming, her determined cheerfulness chasing away any morbid thoughts of a class of stiffs—literally.

The house jobs were quickly filled. Maggie, raising her hand at the right moment, found herself fire marshal, which meant that she had to count to make sure everyone was out of the building when they assembled at the large black oak, the designated meeting place during a drill or the real thing. Before she could slip into a trance of dancing flames and valiant rescues, she heard someone say, "Is it really wise to start the year with a new girl in a position of such responsibility? I mean, she doesn't know anybody. She could easily miss one of us."

It was Marcia, of course. Maggie couldn't think of anything to say, although, exasperatingly, she knew she would come up with any number of retorts later. She had volunteered because she thought she ought to do something and she knew she'd never have the nerve to run for any of the class offices. Let Vicky or Christie do that.

Christie came quickly to her roommate's defense. "She can count, can't she? And I assume a roll call is taken."

"I don't think it matters whether someone is new or not, Marcia. Now, let's see . . . I need someone to distribute notices." Terry continued down the list. Finally, she said, "And last but not least, we need Cabot Guides for the 'Greenies.' Sorry, girls," she apologized at once, "but that's what new girls were called—you know, like greenhorns—until the Cabot Council abolished it a few years ago, and old habits die hard, I guess. Okay, so how many guides do I need? I guess it's just three, since there are no new day girls.''

The room grew silent and everyone looked toward the couch, as they had been off and on since the exchange between Marcia and Christie.

''Now, now, let's not all volunteer at once. You *know* how important this is. Remember what it felt like when you were new.''

Maggie wished a hole in the floor would suddenly open up, turn into a tunnel, and transport her back to Little Bittern. Vicky spoke up. ''We don't really need guides. We've read the handbook and can certainly find our way around ourselves. Please don't trouble yourselves.'' She added this in a voice dripping with sarcasm.

''But new girls always have guides at Cabot.'' Terry's voice was pleading.

''I have only been here one year myself, but I would be happy to be a guide. My name is Marine Collonges,'' a tall, slender girl with a heavy French accent offered from across the room. She pronounced *guide* the French way—*geede*—and there were a few muffled snickers.

''And my sister and I make three.'' An African-American girl cast a defiant look at the girls on the couch. ''My name is Imani Brooks, and this is my sister, Aisha. And yeah, we really are identical twins.'' She smiled and the three newcomers instantly felt better. ''Now, have we earned our goodies, Terry?'' Imani added, her round, pleasant face turned toward the housemother.

''Absolutely. I'm starved, too. But one last thing— don't forget, my door is always open. Come to me if you have any questions, problems, or just want to talk.

I'll post my class schedule. Except for those hours and Sunday afternoon—my time off—I'll be around.''

The girls went into the next room, which had been a dining room. Now it served as a gathering place, and a kitchenette had been added. There were smaller common rooms on the other two floors, as well. Maggie, Christie, and Vicky got some food and started across the room to sit with their guides, who were beckoning to them. Maggie was inclined at this point to think of them as guardian angels. Halfway there, a girl jostled her arm and hot cocoa spilled down her jeans.

"Hey!" Her leg was burning beneath the brand-new pants. She wasn't sure which was causing her eyes to smart with tears—the pain or annoyance at the thought of trying to wash the spot off.

"Oh, sorry. I didn't see you.''

It was the girl who had been sitting next to Marcia on the couch.

And it was no accident.

❖Chapter Three

THE FIRST THEFT WAS ON SUNDAY.

Christie, Maggie, and Vicky were in their room when they heard three sharp blasts from the housemother's police whistle, a pause, then three more. They knew from the handbook and their trusty guides that that meant they should assemble immediately in the living room. Four followed by four meant everyone should leave the house at once, so presumably there wasn't any danger.

"I wonder what's up?" Vicky said. "I didn't notice anything going wrong during the picnic. Maybe it's just some announcements about the first day of classes tomorrow."

The picnic had, in fact, been a great success. Maggie had felt a bit sad at first when she saw all the parent-daughter groups, but ladling out potato salad with Christie to what had seemed like a cast of thousands kept her too busy to dwell on it. Then Aisha and Imani had come to get them to join the others down by the small lake in the middle of the forty-acre campus.

Much of Cabot looked like a park, or a state forest,

Maggie thought as she followed the girls down the path. The school would celebrate its centennial soon, and the buildings represented architectural styles from every era. The grounds had barely changed, only the trees growing taller and even more stately each year; the rhododendrons and other ornamental bushes spilling farther out onto the walks.

Vicky and her parents were sitting on the grass with Marine, listening intently as Imani and Aisha's mother, Mrs. Brooks, described a recent show she had organized for young African-American artists in Boston's South End, where the Brooks family lived. More conversation followed. The group had proved compatible. Vicky had looked around and commented, "You couldn't get much more multicultural than this. We should get that photographer over here and we can be in the next Cabot catalog. You know, 'Cabot prides itself on its diversity.' "

Her father had frowned at his outspoken daughter for a moment, then laughed with everyone else.

"Vive les differences," Marine had said, holding her lemonade glass high.

"It's interesting how those differences are reflected in the variety of names we all have, just in this one group alone," Horace Brooks commented. "Yours, mademoiselle, is French, of course. My wife's first name is Oneida, which is a Native American name."

Oneida Brooks broke in. "It means 'expected' or 'long-awaited.' We also wanted to give our girls names that had some special significance, and we wanted to reflect our African heritage. Imani is Swahili for 'faith' and Aisha means 'life.' Vicky, are you really a Victoria?"

Vicky made a face. The only time her whole name was used was when she was in big trouble.

"Yes, but I like Vicky better." She glanced at her parents, adding, "Much better."

"We, too, searched for a name with meaning for our child," Henry Lee said. "When Vicky was born, it was a victory after years of longing, and we had also just received our immigration documents to come here."

Vicky had never heard this and wondered why not.

"At that time, we also changed our Chinese names to English ones. We were making a fresh start."

This, Vicky had known. Her grandmother still used Henry and Virginia's original names, but she was the only one. Even within the rest of the family, the new names jumped out from the stream of Chinese when they got together and talked. Vicky wondered how it would be to have two names. Which was your real name? When you thought about yourself, which name did you use?

Mrs. Lee had been looking at her husband while he spoke and Vicky could easily read the slight embarrassment in her mother's eyes—revealing family intimacies to strangers—but there was something else there, too: pride. She determined to get her mother alone the next visit home and ask her about some of these things, like the story of Vicky's name. It was so easy for Vicky to talk to everybody else in the world. Why should it be any different with her mother?

Vicky turned toward Christie, about to relate the story of Christie's name, then stopped. The girl was so private. If she wanted to tell the story, she would, but she kept silent.

"I'm Margaret. I looked it up in one of those baby-name books and it means 'pearl' in Greek, but when I asked my mother why they chose it, she said they just liked the way it sounded with Porter.'' Maggie sounded disappointed. She would have liked a name fraught with meaning. ''I'm used to Maggie now, but when I'm older, I'm going to use Margaret. It's more, well, grown-up.''

''We'll call you anything you want,'' Marine offered.

''Maggie is fine. At the moment, Margaret is for when I come home too late, that kind of stuff.''

The weather had cooperated and the sunny afternoon stretched out lazily before them. When the group did slip apart—Marine to search out two other French-speaking girls, ninth graders; the Lees to look at the library and other places they hadn't had time to see before; the Brookses to chat with parents and teachers they knew from prior years—Christie and Maggie stayed put, content to feed the ducks with the remains of their sandwiches.

The ducks reminded Maggie of Terry's slippers. She giggled. ''Terry is certainly not what I imagined our housemother would be like. I was thinking more along the lines of Mrs. Danvers—you know, the housekeeper from Daphne du Maurier's *Rebecca*.''

Maggie's love of mysteries had resulted in a large collection of T-shirts. Today's sported the slogan SO MANY MYSTERIES, SO LITTLE TIME.

Christie nodded. ''Me, too. Especially when I first saw the dorm—you know, the creepy, maybe haunted house in the neighborhood where kids never trick-or-treat.''

Maggie entered into the spirit of the conversation. ''Yeah, and then one day a passerby hears this reedy little voice singing—no, wait, hears two people talking and goes up to the door to investigate, pushes it open, but nobody's there!''

"The possibilities are endless,'' Christie said, ''but, to get back to your point, Terry definitely doesn't match Widow, or my notions of what the housemother would be like. I did know that whoever it was wouldn't be another Hallie—that's the person who's been living with us since my mother got sick.''

Nobody could be like Hallie. Dear, dear Hallie. Hugging her was like squeezing a soft sack of flour, flour that smelled faintly of lavender soap. She was always waiting for Christie at the end of the school day. They'd sit in the kitchen, talking about everything from politics—Hallie followed the intricacies of Boston's races with a fervor that suggested a day at the track rather than the polls—to Christie's diving career. The only thing they didn't talk about was Molly Montgomery, dozing upstairs in the beginning, then a few streets away at Massachusetts General Hospital toward the end. Christie gave her head a little shake. Don't think about it. Don't think about it. This was the mantra she'd composed, and for once it succeeded. "I heard yesterday that Terry was a last-minute replacement. A Miss Donovan—I think that's the name—had been here forever.''

"What happened?'' Maggie asked. "Did she die or something?'' She regretted the words instantly, but then they couldn't avoid the subject of death for the whole year, could they? Christie appeared not to notice. Her mouth curved up mischievously.

"Not exactly. She eloped!''

"How old was she?'' Maggie's usual picture of this romantic escapade was being skewed.

"Forty something. Her mother didn't approve of her boyfriend, so they had to run away. Aisha told me all about it. The girls think it's a hoot. Nobody had a clue."

"Imagine being under your mother's thumb when you're that age! And imagine getting married when you're so old."

"She's been waiting for her lover to come back for over twenty years," one woman whispered to her companion as they watched the lone woman pass by. She was stooped from making beds at the local inn, which was managed by the indomitable matriarch of the family. *"I hear she was jilted at the altar but has always believed he'll come back. Funny, despite her age, her face is still beautiful."* Suddenly, the figure of a man appeared on the horizon. The old woman's steps quickened. It was—

"Terry got hired because Mrs. Babcox knew the family, even before Terry came here as a student." Christie continued the conversation, unaware that her partner was years ahead of her and miles away. "I guess that's why she did come. Anyway, Terry is enrolled at the community college after taking some time off; she wants to get certified to teach science. She was a biology major at college. Cabot was desperate to get somebody, and Terry agreed to take the job until they find a permanent replacement for the wild and woolly former housemother."

Maggie was back. "I hope they don't until the end of the year. She does have a boyfriend, though. Vicky told me. You know, it's amazing how much she's found out about this place. She's a born detective, or spy. Anyway, I hope Terry doesn't elope or get replaced. I'm kind of used to her."

"After three days?" Christie was amused. "But I agree. Besides, the devil you know—"

The rest of her proverb was interrupted by a shout from Vicky on the hill overlooking the lake. "The parents are all leaving. I thought you might want to say good-bye."

They did, and both girls scrambled up the grassy slope.

Mr. and Mrs. Lee had brought boxes of dumplings and other things from the Ginger Jar, so the roommates skipped dinner that night, savoring the feeling of no homework—freedom they wouldn't enjoy again for a long, long time.

The picnic, they all agreed, had been excellent.

Responding to the whistle blasts, the girls quickly made their way downstairs. As she entered the living room, Vicky had a sharp sense of déjà vu. Everyone was sitting in the same places they'd occupied Friday night. Marcia and her court were gathered on the couch, quietly dominating the scene. On Friday night, Vicky had immediately picked up on the influence of that group. As she'd said to herself, It doesn't take a rocket scientist to figure out who's in charge here. If they hadn't been so obvious in their intent to shut the new girls out, Vicky would have been glad to make friends with them. She'd never shied away from making friends with either the "in" group or the "out." Cliques were silly and you got locked into having to do what the others did.

Tonight, there was a sense of tension and agitation in the air. Quiet prevailed, unlike Friday night, when the room had been bursting with chatter, movement—

two girls were showing a third a dance step—and loud laughter.

The housemother was dressed the way she'd been for the picnic—grown-up clothes, in deference to the parents. If Terry had looked like an aging *Sassy* magazine reader before, she now could have stepped from the pages of a Talbot's catalog. She cleared her throat. "I think we're all here. Fire marshal, will you do a count to be sure?"

Maggie was startled. This must be something big. She did a quick count.

"We're all here."

"Thank you." Terry sounded both formal and stern. Maybe it was the clothes. "We have had an unfortunate incident occur. Elaine Feld has had something taken from her room."

There was a collective intake of breath.

"It was a gold bracelet. My grandparents gave it to me when I graduated from elementary school. I'd worn it at the picnic, since they were there with my parents. Then I took it off and left it on my dresser after I changed for dinner. When I came back, it was gone."

"I am going to assume that this was a prank, a big, big mistake, and hope that whoever took it will replace it immediately by leaving it in Ellie's mailbox."

"Why are you assuming it was one of us?" Christie blurted out her thought before she realized it.

"Who else?" Marcia answered, again making it clear who was in charge. "The parents and other guests had all left after the picnic, in case you're thinking of blaming one of our relatives."

Christie turned a dark red. She was angry. "Of course not. But the picnic was catered. They were around a long time packing up the tables and other things. I saw the truck leave about six-thirty. Besides, as we're constantly being warned, it's a big campus and security can't keep track of everyone's comings and goings."

Vicky chimed in. "I think Christie has a point. We have to think of all the possibilities."

Terry looked worried. "Well, in any case, I have to report the theft to Mrs. Babcox and we'll proceed from there. Now, let's see, the house was empty during dinner, so I'll let her know that that's probably when it happened."

The three new girls looked at one another. Maggie started to say something when Tina Wallace, the girl who had spilled cocoa on her, spoke, drawing her words out with poisonous precision. "Not completely empty. I believe our Greenies were having a separate meal here, all by themselves. You know, one of those meals you eat, then a few hours later you're hungry again."

Terry let both the derisive, outmoded term and the undercurrent of racism pass by. "Were you girls here in the house by yourselves? You're supposed to ask me if you plan to skip a meal."

"I'm sorry," Vicky said. She was having trouble keeping herself from running across the room and smacking Tina's smug little Barbie-doll face. The girl was in a "big hair" phase. Really tacky. "My parents brought some food from our restaurant and we ate in the third-floor common room. We didn't know we were supposed to get permission."

"Our fault. We haven't guided them properly. Now they know, and, girl, next time tell your mother and father to bring some for me. The Ginger Jar is my favorite place to eat," Imani said appreciatively.

Vicky recognized the rescue and the intent, but she was still furious.

"I don't like the vibes I'm picking up here," Terry said wearily. "I think everybody had better have lights-out early and do some thinking. Besides, tomorrow you start classes. The reason you're here, remember?"

Back in room thirteen, the new girls hurriedly got ready for bed. All three were steaming.

"I can't believe that Tina! What does she have against us, anyway? Do you think she treats the new girls like this every year?" Maggie asked.

"Tina and Marcia. I bet they were all buzzing about this before the meeting. I'm pretty sure Ellie is their roommate. At least she was in Marcia's room on Friday when I arrived," Christie told them.

"Well, there's nothing we can do about it tonight," Vicky sensibly pointed out. "Tomorrow we'll just have to figure out who the thief is ourselves."

Maggie was excited. It was like one of her daydreams come alive. "Solve the crime ourselves! Of course! We've read enough mysteries. Now what shall we call ourselves? Room Thirteen Detective Agency—no, that's boring."

"The answer is elementary, my dear Sherlock," Vicky said, and pointed to their other roommate. "Who else could we be except Christie and Company?"

The first day of classes for Cabot's eighth graders was not the success it otherwise might have been. It was another sunny Indian summer day. Were it not for a few flashes of red among the swamp maples, fall would have seemed months away. There were no scheduling goofs, two classes in the same room at the same time or students with three English courses and no math. As Mrs. Babcox walked through the buildings, she was pleased. Until she visited the eighth-grade classes, that is. She'd been headmistress at Cabot for over twenty-five years and by now there was little that escaped her notice. She'd heard about the theft and now she saw the results—wrinkled brows, subdued faces, a lack of energy. This, she told herself, better get cleared up soon or it will be a disastrous year. Every Tuesday night, there was a sit-down dinner instead of the usual cafeteria-style one. Teachers and other staff often joined the girls. This Tuesday, Marian Babcox told herself, she'd sit with the eighth grade.

By 3:15, the end of her last class, Christie could hardly wait to get to the pool. She was tired of the looks some girls were giving her, even girls not in her class, and all she could think of was the welcoming water. This was the first day the entire swim team would meet. She changed hurriedly and pushed open the heavy door separating the pool from the locker room. The warm, damp chlorine smell that greeted her instantly lifted her mood and she went over to the coach, Ms. Erica Stevens, with a big smile.

"Glad you're here, Christie. Nice to see you again. Let me introduce you to the others. I want to hear a great big Cabot cheer for our newest member; then we'll warm up and everyone except the divers will get in the water for laps."

The girls gave a mock groan before lustily yelling out, "C-A-B-O-T is the place we want to be! Christie's here, let's give a cheer! C-A-B-O-T!"

"It's how we welcome teams for home meets," Ms. Stevens explained. "Now, L-A-P-S!"

As Christie looked at the group assembled on the long benches, her smile faded. There, at the end, with her long hair pulled up into a cap, was Marcia Lloyd, her younger sister, Jessica, next to her. Both girls were regarding her as something that had come out of the ooze and might as well turn around and go back. Christie squared her shoulders. She'd make friends with the others on the team.

After they'd warmed up, Coach Stevens gathered everyone together again. "I'm afraid I'm going to see that some of you slacked off this summer. Too much beach time without getting wet. Our first meet is only twelve days away, and you'll have to be here every minute you can spare. If I see you on campus and your skin doesn't look like a prune, watch out!"

Everybody laughed. "Now I want the girls who are competing in individual strokes and relays to get in the pool. Tomorrow, we'll work on your starts—everyone's."

Most of the girls dove in the water, and Christie found herself with only ten other girls. "Now let's see how much of what I taught you you've forgotten. Show me a forward dive straight, then tuck, and pike. You all remember that much, I hope."

"She's really a great coach," an older girl whispered to Christie. "Her bark is much worse than her bite."

"Thanks," Christie answered. She needed some encouragement at the moment. Coach Stevens had told her last summer that there was another diver in the eighth grade. But she hadn't told her it was Marcia. Her sister was also among the girls still sitting on the bleachers. She must be terrific to be on the team at her age.

But once Christie was on the board, her mind became

empty and she gave herself over to the feeling she always got as she greeted the empty air—she imagined herself a seabird, diving straight into the water for a fish, leaving scarcely a ripple on the surface.

"Nice, Christie, nice, but you can get higher."

It was Marcia's turn.

"If there was a village on the side of the pool, it would have been destroyed by the tidal wave. Entry, my dear, entry. Your head was buried on your chest."

Some of the team tittered nervously. Christie felt sorry for Marcia. The dive had started out beautifully but ended in an enormous splash. Jessica Lloyd was indeed the youngest member of the team and, Christie soon realized, one of the best. Her dive was flawless— or so it seemed to Christie. "Fair, fair, Jess, but try it again with more concentration. *See* the dive before you do it."

The same girl who'd spoken to Christie before whispered again, "The coach is *very* big on visualization."

"So that's it!" Vicky exclaimed. "Marcia knew there was going to be another diver among the new girls and she didn't want the competition."

Vicky didn't look like a sleuth. She'd layered a bright fuchsia tank top over a French fisherman's blue-and-white-striped T-shirt, adding thin black suspenders that were certainly not necessary to hold up her jeans. She was also wearing an old Timex, tied to her wrist with a leather thong. Her fellow investigators were more soberly dressed in standard-issue oversize T-shirts and jeans—and in Maggie's case, a jean vest. Vicky looked at her two roommates and thought—not for the first time—that she had her work cut out for her. Right away,

43

she had to get Maggie to start using a shampoo with some henna that would bring out the highlights in her hair. It could do with a little trimming too. Maggie refused to part with a single strand, split ends or no split ends, because her mother continued to nag at her to cut it short, saying it's "so easy and you look much cuter." The oversized, thin-rimmed red glasses she wore were perfect, though. Christie always looked good and seemed to be completely unaware of how beautiful she was. Vicky pictured her roommate in a bright yellow top, or royal blue, anything other than the drab colors Christie lived in.

Christie admitted that Vicky's reasoning made sense. "And she probably took Ellie's bracelet herself to make us, specifically me, look bad."

"Not out of the realm of possibility," Vicky agreed. She'd noticed, too, as she went from class to class all day that some girls were giving her a wide berth and whispering remarks as she passed. This was not how Vicky had planned to start her brilliant career at Cabot.

"I don't see any point in confronting her when we don't have any proof yet. We can't go to Terry or Mrs. Babcox, either, without hard facts."

Maggie agreed with Vicky.

"We're at the watch-and-wait stage. Something's bound to happen."

❖Chapter Four

AND IT DID.

But the next development in "The Case of the Missing Gold Bracelet" was not what Christie and Company had been expecting.

Tuesday morning as they were eating breakfast, Ellie came running into the dining hall, waving the bracelet, crying excitedly, "Look, my bracelet! It was in an envelope in my mailbox. I forgot to check yesterday, but I stopped on my way here, and there it was! I'm so happy." Her friends gathered round her and Marcia gave her a big hug.

Maggie, wearing her bright red Sisters in Crime T-shirt today, immediately had two thoughts. One was to wonder what the envelope looked like. Probably the kind you buy in a box at CVS or someplace like that. Impossible to trace. Her other thought was, How could Ellie forget to check her mail? Maggie had been at Cabot for only four days, but her parents and her best friend from home, Charlene, had already written. Not check your mail! Please!

"Watch what happens next," Vicky said in a low voice.

Sure enough, the girls congratulating Ellie soon turned their attention to the new girls. "I'm glad you got it back," Tina said in a loud voice. "It's just a shame it had to happen in the first place. Some people . . ." She let her remark trail off, but the meaning was clear, especially since she was looking directly at the table the new girls occupied.

Christie stood up. "I don't want to be late for French. We can talk at lunch. Who on earth do you suppose took it, and why return it?"

"Guilt—and maybe the fact that it's got Ellie's initials on the front of the band. You wouldn't ever be able to wear it, unless by some weird coincidence yours were the same," Vicky answered.

"But a jeweler can take initials off," Maggie said.

"Yes, but sometimes gold is soft, and the bracelet looked pretty thin. It might not have been possible. That is, if somebody tried."

"You know a lot about this kind of thing." Christie knew very little about the properties of gold jewelry, except that the posts she wore in her pierced ears had to be real, otherwise, she'd get some kind of infection— or her ears would turn green.

"And plan to know more. Don't forget, 'Diamonds are a girl's best friend!' "

The three friend laughed and rushed off to their classes.

Marion Babcox had heard about the return of the bracelet and was relieved. On Tuesday night, the dining hall was lighted by candles, a throwback to earlier days when every night had been like this. Instead of the usual cafeteria-style dinner, tonight's was served by the freshman class, which was assigned to wait on tables. They wore big starched aprons and brought the food to the tables, family-style. It was more formal than other nights and students took a little extra time to comb hair, maybe change clothes in a nod to the past.

Tonight, Mrs. Babcox presided at one of the tables. She had deliberately chosen to sit with the three eighth graders new to Cabot. Grilled chicken was piled high on a platter, surrounded by bowls of steamed vegetables, rice pilaf, and freshly baked rolls. She watched as slender Christie filled her plate, obviously hungry.

Mrs. Babcox smiled. "I can always tell who's going out for sports. You've a diver, if I recall correctly."

"Yes, and it's true. I'm starving by dinnertime." Tonight, she was even hungrier than usual. Somehow, when she'd left the pool, she'd still had energy to burn, and the beauty of this early New England fall—the air fresh and still warm—called to her. There was no way she could sit indoors doing homework, so she went for a long run.

"How about the rest of you? What activities have you selected?" They went around the table, and when it was Maggie's turn, she answered, "I've signed up for the Latin and Astronomy Clubs. I also tried out for the field hockey and volleyball teams, but I won't know if I made either of them until Thursday."

"Latin?" Vicky hadn't realized Maggie was this interested in dead languages. Dead bodies, sure, but what did the Latin Club do?

Mrs. Babcox answered her unspoken question. "I loved studying Latin—and Greek. You'll have a great deal of fun with the club, my dear. They have banquets, complete with togas, and take field trips to look at the antiquities at the Museum of Fine Arts in Boston. Last spring, they staged a reading of the *Trojan Women* by Euripides in our little amphitheater. And what about you, Vicky? Can't we interest you in signing up?''

Vicky made a slight face. ''The acting part would be all right. I joined the Drama Club. We're going to do Arthur Miller's *The Crucible* this semester. Tryouts are tomorrow, and I want to be one of the girls who imagines she's possessed and falsely accuses people.''

''A dangerous thing,'' murmured Mrs. Babcox. The girls around the table looked uncomfortable. She changed the subject quickly. ''Anything else?''

''I tried out for soccer and I'm volunteering to be in the group that reads at the nursing home. It seemed like a good thing to do. I guess I miss my grandmother. She's always lived with us.'' It wasn't until she said it out loud that Vicky realized she really did miss her grandmother. She'd seen more of her than any other adult. Alternately scolding and praising, her grandmother was a constant. Vicky didn't like to think how old Mrs. Lee was, or how frail. She has many, many years, Vicky told herself firmly.

''I was very close to one of my grandmothers also. The other died when I was young. Now I'm a grandmother myself! I think going to the nursing home is a fine thing to do. Now I'm going to switch to another table for dessert. It's been a pleasure joining you.''

The girls stood up as Mrs. Babcox left. She was feeling much better about the future course of Cabot's eighth grade.

Of course, she hadn't been there late that afternoon when the class held elections.

Day students and boarders gathered in the living room

at Widow. Terry had a class, so Mr. Pritchard, one of the English teachers, was running the meeting.

"Now, you all know how this works. Let's have nominations. The voting will be by secret ballot."

"He seems to be in a hurry," Maggie whispered to Christie. "Maybe he's got a date." The two girls giggled. Mr. Pritchard was the image of an old-fashioned schoolmaster, an Ichabod Crane. His Adam's apple was so big, Maggie noted, that it was a wonder he could swallow. She couldn't keep her eyes from following the way it moved up and down as he spoke or cleared his throat, which was often. She bit the inside of her cheek. She was starting to laugh.

"Can you give us some idea of what influenced your work, particularly the sharp-edged, comedic portrayal of the schoolteacher in your most recent book?" Since the announcement of the Nobel Prize in Literature, reporters had been following her every footstep. She tried to duck into the limo waiting for her at the curb. "Please, Ms. Porter, one more question—"

"Let's start at the top. Nominations for class president, please, ladies." Maggie snapped to attention.

There was dead silence in the room. Tina Wallace raised her hand. "I nominate Marcia Lloyd." Seconds came from all over the room.

"Further nominations?" Silence again. Vicky was seriously annoyed. Wasn't anyone going to challenge Marcia? She could nominate Christie or Maggie, but it would be pointless. She looked over at Aisha and Imani and raised an eyebrow. Would one of them run? They both shrugged and almost imperceptibly shook their heads.

49

"All right, if that's your pleasure. Let's move on to vice president."

It was the same thing, except this time it was Tina who ran unopposed.

And on down the list: secretary, treasurer, and the four class representatives to the Cabot Council, the student government.

"Well, you certainly made my job easy." Mr. Pritchard rubbed his hands together. "Congratulations to the new officers. I know the eighth grade will have a super year." And then he was out of there.

"I thought we were going to talk about next weekend's overnight," Vicky said to Marine as the girls got up and moved about the room.

"We have to wait for Terry. But it's pretty simple. We leave early Saturday morning and come back late Sunday night. I've never done the Outward Bound program, but I understand it involves teaching you how to depend on and trust each other to survive."

Vicky looked around at her fellow classmates. "Great. Piece of cake. No problem." Then she added to herself a resounding *Not!*

The next two days flew by. The girls were constantly on the go and had barely time to tell one another any news.

"I can't believe how much homework I have," Maggie complained. "Do you think they're piling it on because we'll be gone this weekend, or is it always going to be like this?"

The girls were in their room, getting ready for bed.

"I'm afraid it's always going to be like this, and fitting in enough practice time before next week means getting up even earlier. I want to go this weekend, but I hate to lose those two days,'' Christie complained.

Vicky was looking through her clothes, thinking of what to wear. Of the three of them, she was spending the least time on her subjects. She was afraid if she thought about it too hard, her ability to do schoolwork might easily vanish into thin air. She'd been expected to do well for as long as she could remember and she had. People sometimes told her she was smart, but there was a part of her that worried she was fooling the world. She just had . . . well, a knack.

"Too 'in your face' for Cabot?" She held up a short black dress with tiny polka dots and spaghetti straps. "Of course, I'd wear it over tights and a shirt."

"Wear it," Christie advised. "You can get away with it. I'd look like I'd suddenly been possessed by Madonna."

"You could at least wear brighter colors," Vicky advised. Here was her chance. "When we go into town together, I'll take you to my two favorite places: Filene's Basement and the Goodwill store."

Maggie got into bed. She wasn't paying much attention to her roommates; she was thinking about the scene she'd unwittingly observed early in the afternoon. She'd told Christie and Vicky about it over dinner, but it was still playing vividly in her mind.

The first floor at Widow had a small study room off the old dining room, now the common room. The study was mostly used by day students, but Maggie liked its coziness and had discovered she could concentrate better there than in the big library with so many people around or in her room, which had too many potential distractions. She had had an hour before her last class and, seeing that the room was empty, decided to study there. She threw open the window to let the sunny autumn day in and started translating Virgil's *Aeneid.* *"Arma, virumque cano."* "I sing of arms, and the man." It was the story of Aeneas escaping from fallen Troy and traveling to new lands. She was soon lost in the epic poem.

"Don't tell me what to do! Since when did you get to be in charge?" It was a man's voice and he was angry. Maggie couldn't hear the reply, although there was one. It sounded like a woman, and the answer was muffled by tears.

"Look, maybe it would be better if we just split. Okay?" His voice was very matter-of-fact. He could have been talking about the latest weather report.

Maggie crept over to the window, crouched down, and peered over the sill. The woman was Terry, her housemother, and the man must be her boyfriend! It wasn't really ethical to eavesdrop, but Maggie hadn't planned to—and they *were* talking in a public place.

"No." Terry's voice was clear, although she had been crying. Maggie could see her face now. "Okay, you need your space. I need mine, too. But we don't have to break up to get it." There was a pleading note in her voice. Poor Terry, was all Maggie could think. But then, couples fought. Even her parents had been known to exchange an angry word or two—but not often, and Maggie had never seen her mother cry during an argument. At the movies, yes, but never over things such as who forgot to order the firewood or the increasingly popular, "You always take her side"—"her" being Maggie; "You" being her father. She smiled guiltily and took another look out the window.

The couple was embracing passionately and Maggie quickly ducked down. Well, at least everything was all right—for now. Terry's boyfriend looked older than she was, but that wasn't hard. He was extremely good-looking. Maggie definitely approved. He had long—but not too long—dark brown wavy hair, and a great body. He was wearing jeans, a crisp-looking yellow oxford-cloth shirt, and Top-Siders. Maybe he was a sailor. Another plus. Maggie loved to sail. She looked again. He was holding Terry at arm's length. Maggie could see where Terry's face had rumpled his shirt.

"Now let's get going. Give me a smile."

Terry's face could have lighted up all Broadway.

They walked back to Terry's car, which was parked in the garage, got in, and pulled out.

It was hard to get back to Virgil.

Maggie made field hockey but not volleyball. Vicky got the role of Mary Warren in the play, but she did not make the soccer team.

"I thought I was good, not great, but these girls are something else! I'm fast, though, so I went to talk to one of the phys ed teachers and I'm going to do intramural track."

Both Christie and Maggie decided to join Vicky in the nursing-home project. But the main topic of eighth-grade conversation was the upcoming weekend trip.

At lunch, the girls were sitting with their Cabot Guides. Everyone was laughing.

"I don't know whether it's the idea of seeing a male under the age of eighty or not hitting the books for two days that's got me all excited," Aisha said.

"Two guesses," teased her sister. "Aisha met a certain someone when we were on vacation this summer and he just so happens to be starting eighth grade at Mansfield."

"So there's at least one new eighth grader over there," Christie commented.

"I'd be surprised if he was the only one. It's a bigger school—nice ratio for us—so there are always more new kids."

Vicky had met some of the Mansfield boys during *The Crucible* tryouts. She had her eye on Mark Reese, a tenth grader who was going to play the lead, John Proctor. His reading had electrified everyone watching. She didn't want to say anything to the group, though. He would probably never even look at an eighth grader, even one as fearless as Vicky.

"What happens if the weather's bad?" From the moment Maggie had heard that they were going to the Cape—possibly see the ocean—she could hardly wait. After Little Bittern, Cabot felt very landlocked.

"We go anyway. It's all part of the survival thing."

"Let's pray for sunshine."

Saturday morning dawned sunny but cool. Vicky pulled her blanket up. "I'm not exactly looking forward to roughing it in subzero temperatures. Couldn't they find some way for us all to bond indoors?" Nature girl she was not.

Christie and Maggie ruthlessly pulled the covers off their roommate. "We have exactly thirty minutes to shower and get to breakfast. I'm taking a chance that Terry won't have someone do room inspection while we're gone and leaving this mess," Christie said. "Beat you to the bathroom!" Vicky jumped from her bed but

Christie had her towel and things already assembled. She was out the door before Vicky could find her slippers.

Maggie was drying her hair by the mirror. "At least we don't have to pack."

To save time, all students, day and boarding, had been asked to place their knapsacks in the first-floor study room by eight o'clock the night before. They'd be stowed on the buses while the girls were eating breakfast.

Soon the three girls were running out the front door, almost colliding with Mr. Pritchard, who was leaving, too.

"I hope he's not one of the chaperones," Maggie said as soon as they were out of earshot. "I'd be imagining his Adam's apple getting caught in the ropes course or something else like that and end up making a fool out of myself instead."

Vicky and Christie laughed. "He doesn't strike me as the outdoors type," Vicky said. "I'm sure he'd much rather read *War and Peace* or something back here. I wonder what he was doing at the dorm? Maybe Terry's ditched her boyfriend."

"Beauty for the Beast? I don't think so." Maggie was quite definite. "I saw the guy, remember, and he was not someone you'd get rid of for Mr. Pritchard. Besides Mr. P. is ancient and probably married."

"I didn't see a ring when he was running the elections," Christie observed. "But then, lots of men don't like to wear wedding bands."

"You really are a sleuth. I never noticed anything like that about him." Maggie was admiring.

"He also had a hole in the heel of his sock that you

could see when he crossed his legs. Another sign of no wife?'' Christie continued.

''Or a very busy wife,'' Vicky offered. ''*My* husband is going to have to be responsible for his own clothes.''

The three girls entered the dining hall. An unusual sight greeted their eyes: boys, lots of boys. Aisha called out to them, ''We saved you some seats. Hurry up!'' She returned to what was obviously a very important conversation with the boy next to her. ''Must be the summer honey,'' Maggie whispered to Christie.

The girls went through the line and sat down.

''We think we forgot to tell you about the traditional Mansfield-Cabot breakfast,'' Marine said with chagrin. ''I'm sorry, because now there isn't much time.''

''We're going to be together the whole weekend,'' Vicky reassured her, smiling at one of the boys at the table.

''Christie Montgomery! Is there anyone named Christie Montgomery here?'' A tall boy with large hands and feet that he still seemed to be growing into stood at the end of the table. He started to call her name again, but Christie got up quickly, her cheeks flushed, and went over to him. Twice was enough. What could he possibly want?

''I'm Christie,'' she said.

''Hi, I'm Scott Franklin. I saw you dive last spring at the Regionals. You were fantastic. I dive, too, but we're not in the same ballpark. Which sounds pretty stupid, but 'in the same pool' would have sounded even dumber. Anyway, you know what I mean.'' He smiled, an easy, self-assured smile, the smile of someone who was used to being liked and, Christie thought, hadn't ever had anything bad happen to him.

"Thank you," she said, "but I think you're mistaken. I know I heard your name read off during the awards."

"Pretty far down—but this year's going to be different. Anyway, I just wanted to get to know you. Cabot's lucky to have you on the team. And since we travel to most of the same meets, we're going to be seeing a lot of each other."

Christie felt a little breathless. Scott was not only cute; he was actually interested in *her*.

"Well, I have to go. Maybe we'll be on the same bus."

Christie nodded. "Nice to meet you." Nice to meet you! Yuck! It sounded like something you said to one of your parents' friends. He must really think I'm a jerk, she thought.

"Nice to meet you, too." He smiled right into her eyes.

When she got back to the table, Imani said, "Well, the great Scott Franklin! What was that all about?"

"He's a diver, too. We were at the same meet last spring."

"And he just couldn't get you out of his mind. Not bad, girl. He's got looks *and* brains."

Christie wished Imani would stop talking. Some of the boys at the table had overheard, and she didn't want anything to get back to Scott. She didn't want to seem overeager—or not eager enough.

Her dilemma was solved by a frantic voice. "It's gone! Completely gone. My CD player and all my money!"

It was Marcia and she was talking to Terry, who was sitting at a table with some of the staff from both Cabot and Mansfield.

"Now, calm down, Marcia. What's happened?"

"They haven't loaded the knapsacks on the buses because they're late. I saw mine sticking up and decided I wanted my portable CD player for the trip down. It's not there, nor is the twenty dollars I put into the inside zippered compartment."

"Did you look in your room? You might have left it there. And as for the money, how about searching your pockets?" Terry looked at the other adults with a pained expression that indicated how she regarded Marcia's outburst.

Marcia's voice became steely. She intended to be taken seriously. "I've looked in my room. I've looked in my pockets—*all* my pockets. I've even talked to my sister in case she borrowed it without asking." Her voice was level and patronizing. "It's clearly been stolen. Like the bracelet." Dead silence filled the room. Someone dropped a knife on an empty plate and the noise was startlingly loud. Marcia raised her voice, turned, and firmly repeated the accusation. "Stolen." She was directly facing the table where Christie and Company sat as still as everyone else. "Stolen," Marcia said one last time, emphatically.

It was starting all over again.

❖Chapter Five

IT SEEMED AS IF ALL THE EIGHTH GRADERS at Cabot and Mansfield Hill were looking at them, specifically at her, Christie thought as she stood in line to get on the bus. The day—no, wait, the whole weekend was totally ruined. She knew how it would be, just as before. No direct accusation, but lots of innuendo. Scott was ahead of her. He turned and their eyes met briefly. He looked puzzled. She thought he shrugged his shoulders slightly, but she couldn't be sure. Anyway, what did it mean? She wouldn't know until they had had a chance to talk, and that might not ever happen again. She'd seen Marcia and Tina, the centers of attention, in the middle of a large group of Mansfield guys.

Vicky poked her in the back.

"Cheer up. We know we didn't do it—if, in fact, her stupid CD player has been stolen. I intend to forget about the whole thing and have a good time this weekend."

Maggie heard what Vicky said. "Spitting in the wind" is what they called it on Little Bittern. She felt the way Christie looked. They were outsiders again.

Their Cabot Guides had gone off with their own friends, either forgetting about the new girls or ... Maggie shook her head. She knew Aisha, Imani, and Marine believed they were innocent. Oh, why did this have to happen? For a moment, she thought she had said it out loud. People were looking at her oddly.

"Hey, space cadet, get on the bus!" Maggie laughed in relief and embarrassment. She hadn't realized the line was moving. The boy who had called out to her was making circles next to his head, but he wasn't mocking her unkindly.

"Crazy," he said with a broad grin.

"I'm afraid so," she called back over her shoulder. Maybe the weekend wouldn't be so bad after all.

The seats on the bus were for two, and Christie found herself next to an eighth grader from Cabot who was already busy chatting to her friends across the aisle. Christie changed to the window seat so the girl wouldn't be lying in her lap the whole trip. Vicky and Maggie were several rows ahead and Scott was near the rear. She turned around, but he was looking the other way and didn't see her. Mercifully, Marcia was on the other bus. Christie slumped down as they pulled out into the drive leading away from the campus and tried to think of other things—of the meet, of her roommates.

She had been lucky. They were great, but totally different from her, she thought. For one thing, they were so sure about things. Yeah, Maggie was shy and worried about her glasses and the braces that were going on her teeth soon. There had been no feasible way to have them put on while she lived on the island and her mother was insistent they be done, Maggie'd told them, bewailing her fate as virtually the only "metal-mouthed" eighth grader. "If only Mom wouldn't keep saying, 'You'll thank me someday.' It's today that matters!" But that was all on the surface. Maggie had told Christie the first night that she wanted to be a writer and probably an English professor, too, since she had been told it was hard for writers to support themselves. She kept a journal and wrote in it religiously every day. "The only way to be a writer is to write," she'd said seriously. Even Vicky, who had seemed at the beginning to be interested only in clothes and her very pretty face and hair, had already decided she wanted to get a doctorate in environmental chemistry and do research. She'd spent the summer before in a lab at MIT in a special program for young students interested in scientific careers.

Christie didn't have a clue about where she was going. Some days when she woke up, she wasn't even sure where she was now.

She felt herself slipping down the tunnel. She tried the mantra, Don't think about it. Don't think about it.

It didn't work.

One Christmas when she had been eight, her mother had gotten her a red plaid skirt and a matching red sweater with a black Scottie in the middle, a shiny brass chain stitched on as a collar. Christie had hated the outfit and told her mother it was dumb, for babies, and that she, Christie Montgomery, would never, never wear it. Her mother had carefully folded it back into the box, tears in her eyes. Christie looked out the bus window, her head pounding. I'm sorry, Mom. I'm so sorry. Mom. Mom. Please come back, Mom.

"We have time for a couple of exercises before lunch. After you eat, we'll start the hard stuff," an energetic dark-haired young woman told the group when they had all gotten off the bus and stretched. "Don't worry, you won't be sitting down. First, we've got to break up into smaller groups. Four should do it."

Maggie looked around. It wasn't Maine, but it was beautiful. They were in a large, open field surrounded by woods on three sides. The ocean was within earshot. She could hear the waves and the cries of seagulls. The meadow gave way to sand and dune grass on one side. She hoped there would be a chance to walk on the beach. She forced herself to pay attention to what the woman was saying. Maggie wasn't sure she was going to enjoy all these exercises. She knew they were designed to bring the group together, to build trust. Little did these people know what an impossible task they had.

Christie was next to her. She seems as tuned out as I am sometimes, Maggie thought. She turned to her friend and asked anxiously, "Are you okay?"

"Fine," Christie muttered, confirming Maggie's suspicions that she was anything but.

"Okay, start counting."

Too late, Maggie realized that she and Christie would be in different groups since they were standing next to each other. "Two," she said dismally. "Three," Christie said softly. Vicky, on Christie's other side, was a four. Maggie watched breathlessly as the kids counted off. Who was going to be with Marcia? Maybe luck would be with them and Marcia would be a one. She thought she was number one, anyway. It fit. Luck was not with them and Marcia was a four. Maggie was happy that at least Christie wouldn't have to be with her. Her roommate seemed depressed and in no mood to handle what would surely be poisonous looks and sly remarks from Marcia.

"Now, each group take a corner on the field and we'll get started."

Group four's leaders were Linda and Tom. The first thing they told everyone was to circle up.

"We need eye contact. You can't communicate without it, so when you hear 'circle up,' form a tight circle wherever you are," Tom explained. "And remember, we're here to have fun, besides maybe learning a thing or two about ourselves and one another."

The first exercise was called Saucers. Linda and Tom placed knotted rope circles of varying sizes on the ground; they were spread pretty far apart. "The object of this game is to help one another, pure and simple," Linda said. She was tall and had a long ponytail tied at the base of her neck with a bright red bandanna. "When we say, 'Change,' run to another circle. You can't be in the same one twice in a row, and all feet have to be within the circle."

This shouldn't be too difficult, Vicky thought. She heard the command and ran for the nearest circle. It was a small one and the other occupant was a Mansfield boy with an unfortunate complexion. He seemed genuinely delighted to be part of a pair. In Vicky's old school, the kids divided themselves into four basic groups: the popular kids, the middles, the rejects, the total rejects. She was afraid this boy would have been near the bottom of the food chain, but at the moment, so was she. She'd never stuck to any of the groups anyway, moving in and out of all of them.

"Change!" Vicky gave her circle mate a smile and

raced off to a larger circle she had spotted earlier. Except it wasn't there! Linda and Tom had removed some of them after the first command. Vicky squeezed into a laughing group struggling to keep all feet within the rope.

"Change again!"

Vicky dashed madly for a circle, almost colliding with two Cabot girls.

"Help each other! Help each other!" Tom and Linda urged, the ropes looped over their arms.

Vicky looked at the group of twenty-five kids. How were they ever going to fit into the remaining circles?

"Lie down!" shouted Ellie Feld. "Only your feet have to be in, right?"

They made it through several more runs; then there were only two circles left, then one. Vicky found herself sitting down on the grass next to Marcia, their feet inside the rope. "Quick, get closer! We can make it!" She grabbed Vicky's arm, pulling her tight to make room for another person. Maybe these games do perform miracles, Vicky thought, or maybe Marcia's Cabot team spirit was so strong that she was willing to forget her personal enmities—for the duration.

"You guys are great!" Tom enthused. "Remember there are no winners and no losers in these cooperative games. You have to depend on every single person in the group."

Christie's group had started with the same exercise. She had been struggling to pull herself out of the depression that had engulfed her on the bus. She felt as if she were swimming underwater and that the surface was still a long way above. Just as she thought her lungs might burst and she might faint, she felt a hand on her shoulder. "We're supposed to go over to those trees."

It was Scott. She let out her breath and drew a deep mouthful of air. She wasn't going to pass out this time.

As they walked to the spot where the leaders were waiting, the excited talk around her was lifting her spirits. It was a gorgeous sunny day. Everyone was already stripping off sweatshirts and sweaters. She looked gratefully at Scott. He seemed to have sensed something was wrong. She may have imagined it, but she thought he had given her an extra hug when they were all piling into the rope circles.

One of their leaders, Annie, was explaining the next task. "This is called Turnstile. Jake and I will be turning this long jump rope. You've got to get the whole team from one side to the other. But the rope can never be empty. If it is, you go back and start all over again.

"No problemo," a Mansfield boy said. "Come on, guys." The rope started to turn, slowly but inexorably. In ones and twos, the kids ran under to the other side. They were almost there. Only one boy was left.

"I can't do it. It looks like it's going to slice me in two."

"Oh, for goodness sake, it's only a jump rope," Tina said in exasperation. "You messed us up."

The leaders hung back for a moment. Scott looked at Tina. "Don't tell me there aren't things that freak you out. And besides, we're a team. Come on back to the other side and let's make a plan."

"Why doesn't he go first with someone? I'll go," Christie said. "If you do something right away, you don't have time to get nervous. Or at least that's how it is for me when I dive. I always love it when I'm first or early on in the order.''

"Great," someone said.

They tried it, but this time a group of four, including Tina, got tangled in the rope.

"There's got to be a better way," Aisha said. "To keep the rope full, let's have somebody jump the rope until everybody's through. Now, who's the best jumper?"

"Definitely Peter—he's our track star. The man sails over the hurdles."

Peter looked a little embarrassed, but he took his place and started jumping. Christie went through with her charge and everyone followed. Peter skipped out and Annie and Jake burst into applause.

"I really liked what I saw you doing there," Annie said. "No one got scapegoated, although it was a possibility for a moment, but you worked through it and came up with a plan. You listened to one another."

"Active listening," Jake stressed, "not the 'Oh, yeah, I heard you, Mom or Dad' kind." Everybody laughed.

"And now that you're doing so well together, we're going to split you up again. Two groups. Start counting."

This time, Christie had her wits about her and quietly slipped one away from Scott.

When they broke for lunch, Christie and Company quickly sought one another out as soon as they'd grabbed their brown bags.

"It's amazing," Maggie said. "I thought the whole idea sounded pretty dumb, but my group is really a group now. You can't do this stuff without working together, and we've been laughing so much that everybody seems like old friends. Our leaders said we were unusually silly. But the way they were saying it was a compliment."

"My group has gotten pretty tight, too," Christie commented. "Although in the beginning, Tina and a few others were really negative. But they're as much into it as anybody now. How about your group? Is Marcia being a jerk?"

"Marcia was born a jerk," Vicky answered. "In the beginning, she was trying to take charge as usual, but she's so competitive and wants her group to do stuff the fastest and best that I think she's called a truce for the weekend. Also, not everyone lets her get away with the Madam President number, which is why I still can't understand why nobody ran against her, or her buddies. We definitely have to do something about that next year!"

"Absolutely. As for now, maybe these exercises give people the courage to stand up to her," Maggie offered.

"Whatever," Christie said. "I'm just glad I'm not in her group. Trust Falls are next and nothing in this world or the next would induce me to fall backward into Marcia Lloyd's arms. Group spirit or no group spirit."

"Lucky me," Vicky said glumly.

"Okay, everybody understand? We can't move on to the other stuff until you've learned to spot each other. Now pair off. Try to choose someone you don't know."

That's easy, Christie thought, looking around. She was about to walk up to a girl in her English class who'd seemed nice when a voice behind her said, "We don't really know each other well. At least not yet." It was Scott. And it was a line, but Christie didn't care. She had a partner.

Jake continued the instructions. "Feet together. Cross your arms over your chest and close your eyes. Remember, spotters, one foot backward for stability. Now start." All around her, Christie heard voices saying what they had been taught: "Spotter ready?" "Yes." "Ready to fall." "Fall Away." She willed herself to drop backward into Scott's waiting arms but found herself frozen to the ground. She opened her eyes in panic.

Annie came over. "Scott, stand a little nearer to Christie and let her feel how close your hands are to her back."

It was only a couple of inches. Christie took a deep breath. I can do this, she thought.

"Don't worry, I'm right here."

She let her breath out and fell—with her eyes open.

By the time they came to the Zipper, Vicky felt as if she could drop from the Empire State Building into the waiting arms of any one of the group, even Marcia's.

"In the Zipper, we form two lines facing each other," Linda called out. "Stand as close as you can to the person next to you. We want the lines tight. Now reach across to the person opposite you, holding your arms at waist level. Alternate your hands with his or hers. Get it? It should look just like a zipper, hence the name." She grinned.

The group stood perpendicular to the side of a low section of bleachers.

"Who wants to be first?" Tom asked.

For a moment, the group was quiet; then the boy who had been in the initial Saucer circle with Vicky earlier stepped forward. "Way to go, Ludwig," the other Mansfield boys cheered.

"Just watch my hands, guys. As soon as I can afford it, I plan to have them insured by Lloyd's of London."

"Pianist, right? Ludwig, as in van Beethoven?" Vicky asked a boy across from her.

"Right. I don't even remember what our Ludwig's real name is anymore. David, I think."

"Okay, Ludwig, you'll be fine," Linda said. "Just don't bend. When you stay straight, your weight is evenly distributed on the spotters. Now climb up there, shake your precious hands together, and twist your arms into your chest so your elbows don't stick out. Then fall away."

Ludwig mounted the bleachers and did as he was told. Before giving the commands, he glanced at the group and proclaimed, " 'It is a far, far better thing that I do, than—' "

He was greeted with cries of "Get the lead out!" and "Be real!" For a moment, Vicky wondered if the act meant he really was apprehensive, but he dropped perfectly with no hesitation. Ludwig, who she'd decided was pretty cool—it wasn't his fault his hormones were attacking his face—was an accomplished performer, and an accomplished ham.

One after another, they fell into the arms of the group. Vicky found it exhilarating and wished she could do it again. They were about to move on to the next activity when Linda said, "Wait, Marcia, we skipped you. Sorry."

"That's okay. I mean, if we're running out of time, I don't have to go."

"Oh yes you do," the boy who'd told Vicky about Ludwig said. "We don't want you to miss out."

Marcia mumbled something. "Sorry," Tom said, "I didn't catch that."

"I don't really want to do it," Marcia said softly.

She's frightened, or she doesn't trust us—or both, Vicky realized.

"Nobody has to do it," Linda reassured her. "But you went through all the other exercises, and I think you won't find it that different. You can stand on a lower step if you want."

Marcia looked around the group. Yes, Vicky noted, there was fear in her eyes, and she felt sorry for the girl.

"All right, I'll try. Once."

"We're all here. It's impossible to hit the ground," Vicky told her. Marcia ignored her. Vicky decided to be charitable and assume that Marcia was preoccupied with her fears.

As Vicky looked up at Marcia's back, she knew that she would catch her and hold her, but she would never, ever like her.

"Fall away!"

Marcia fell, jackknifing her body, and the group pushed together, straining to hold her.

"You almost dropped me!" she screamed.

"No, you didn't stay straight!"

"Circle up!" Tom and Linda called out simultaneously.

"What happened here?" Linda asked when they'd formed the circle and sat down.

"Marcia won't admit she was afraid. She bent and her weight fell on the kids in front."

"Does she have to say she's afraid?" Tom looked at each group member.

"No," Ludwig said. "It's not important. We caught her. She's learned she's safe with us even if she messes up herself in some way. Not that I'm saying you did, Marcia. Besides, I'll bet a lot of us were afraid, or at least uneasy."

That drew some agreement and Marcia stopped pulling at the grass. There was a pile of tufts that she'd been angrily assembling since sitting down.

"I was afraid. I was even afraid when we did the falls on the ground. But you're right—you did catch me. I'm still in one piece and ready for what's next, so long as I can keep my eyes open."

Everybody laughed. Tom and Linda seemed satisfied and the group was together again.

Shadows were beginning to lengthen by the time they approached the final activity, the Wall. All the groups had come back together to watch one another conquer the ten-foot plywood challenge. Maggie's group was the last to go.

"We should do this in no time. We've seen everybody else's mistakes," she said to the girl next to her.

"I don't know. It looks a whole lot taller close-up," the girl replied warily.

"Huddle, huddle!" The group got together and tried to come up with a plan.

"All the short people up first; then they can stand on the platform behind the wall and pull the rest over."

"But how will they reach?"

"Tallest last."

"Who's the tallest?"

Back and forth they went until one boy said, "Let's just do it!" and they broke from the huddle, shouting,

"Do it! Do it!" One by one, they got hauled or boosted over to the other side. Maggie found herself standing on someone's hands, shoved up against the wall, reaching for an arm extended from the top.

"There's only room for one more in the lifeboat! I want you to take it, my darling." He was firm and the expression in his eyes brooked no refusal. Besides, she had to think of the child. She looked over the side. The angry sea roiled below and the tiny white craft was pitching and tossing in the waves like a cork. The howling wind almost drowned out his final words. "Grab my arm. I'll lower you down. You must make haste, but first one last good-bye...."

"Grab on! Grab on!" It was Tina and she was yelling at Maggie to hurry. "We want to beat the other groups' times! Hurry up!" Maggie grabbed and scrambled up. Safely on the platform, she turned to thank Tina, who still held her arm in a viselike grip, not unlike Wonder Woman's. Before she could say a word, though, Tina gave her a vicious pinch before pushing Maggie toward the ladder to climb down. "Get going! You're in the way!"

So much for bonding, Maggie thought sadly as she reached the ground. She wanted to believe that in the heated competition of the moment, Tina had not singled her out, but she knew an intentional pinch when she felt one. She had a little brother after all.

Everyone was tired after the day's exercises. An early bonfire on the beach following supper marked the official end of the day. It was beautiful—the flames reflecting in the dark water; sparks racing toward a sky that seemed immense, a tent filled with a slim crescent moon and stars stretching as far as the eye could see. The chaperones were mellow. One of the teachers from Mansfield had brought a guitar and was getting the kids to sing the kinds of songs everybody's parents liked so much from the sixties and seventies. Instead of protesting, as she would have at home the moment her mother went to put on her James Taylor album for the eleven hundredth time, Maggie found herself joining in. She certainly knew the words.

They piled back on the buses for the campground. There was strict segregation between boys and girls now. Ludwig, who was evidently trying for class clown as well as "most likely to succeed," had tried to hide on the Cabot bus but was quickly booted off.

Once again, the trio wasn't sitting together, but this time they didn't mind being separated. Marcia had been mercifully quiet about the theft and there was a feeling of well-being among the eighth graders.

It didn't last. Reunited with their knapsacks at the campground, a number of the girls discovered things were missing—mostly money.

The chaperones tried to calm everyone down, but despite the day's activities, trust was a scarce commodity. None of the new girls was missing anything, but they had obeyed instructions and not brought anything valuable. Each had a few dollars and some change for an emergency and that was it.

Christie made her way to the bathroom with her roommates.

"I'm so beat, I can't even think about this now. It's like someone is doing this deliberately to set us up. But when could someone have gotten to the knapsacks? We've been together all day."

"But not last night." Vicky was thinking out loud. "The thefts had to have happened back at Cabot when everything was piled in the study."

"Which means it could have been anyone in the school."

"Or Mansfield, for that matter, or the whole town of Aleford," Christie exploded. "Maybe the whole state of Massachusetts!" She felt herself falling back into the earlier depression that had claimed her on the bus ride.

"Hey, don't let this get to you. That's just what they want." Vicky's mouth was set in a firm line. "When we get back to school, we'll figure this out. Now I, for one, want to get to sleep."

They quickly found their places and settled down for the night.

Maggie sighed and snuggled down into the sleeping bag that had been provided. Her toes were cold. She slid her feet as far in as possible and instantly brought them up.

There was something in her bag! Something thin and slimy! A snake! She started to scream, swallowed hard, and carefully got out of the bag.

It was too much of a coincidence that there was a snake in her sleeping bag. Obviously, someone had put it in, someone from Cabot. It would be a harmless snake, unless the girls she suspected were both braver and more resourceful than she thought.

She turned on her flashlight and unzipped the side—slowly.

Soon her beam caught the shiny, glossy diamond-patterned snakeskin. A shiny, glossy diamond-patterned *plastic* snakeskin.

Now she didn't want to scream. She wanted to

laugh—hysterically. It was just like one of Willy's, the kind that he liked to leave on chairs, in the bread box, wherever his mother might chance to be unnerved by it. Uncharacteristically, her mother, the woman who had taken on New York cabbies, currently dealt with impossible guests, and could leap small buildings in a single bound, always reacted with the kind of screech dear to a ten-year-old boy's heart.

Vicky and Christie hadn't noticed what was going on and Maggie decided to wait until the morning to clue them in. Christie had seemed pretty upset by the discovery of the new thefts, and Vicky was right—there was nothing they could do until the next day.

Maggie removed her little friend and tucked it away in her knapsack. Who knew when it might come in handy? She was cheered by that thought. Yet, another less comforting one lurked persistently just below the surface.

Christie and Company was still a target.

❖Chapter Six

THEY'D RETURNED TO CABOT EXHAUSTED—
both physically and emotionally. A fragile trust, how-
ever, had been reestablished on Sunday, nourished by
the Mansfield students, who clearly had no suspicions
of anyone. They turned the thefts into an elaborate
guessing game they called "Sherlocking", posing outra-
geous theories and suspects, including Cabot's headmistress and their headmaster. The boys pictured them as
desperate for cash to escape the schools and head for
Acapulco.

Maggie was not surprised when Tina asked her how
she'd slept, and she told her roommates that there was
obvious disappointment on Miss Perfect's face when
Maggie replied, "Like a baby."

Christie had had a restless night, plagued with dreams
she could not remember.

Vicky had not slept well, either, pointing out that the
ground was not her idea of a mattress.

Back at the dorm, Maggie headed straight for the
mailboxes and gleefully grabbed her mail, racing upstairs to read it in the privacy of room thirteen.

Not expecting anything, Christie was surprised to see mail in hers. Maybe her dad? Her grandparents? She picked up an envelope. But there was no name on the front. No address. No stamp. Probably a notice from one of the clubs or something about diving.

She opened it and the letters, crudely cut out from magazines, hit her face-on.

EveRy onE KNOws YoU'rE GUILTy.
COnFesS BefOre iT's ToO LaTE.

Christie gasped and dropped the letter as if it had singed her fingertips. The girl next to her asked if everything was okay. It was Ellie Feld.

"Yes," Christie stammered as she stooped down to pick up the note, which she quickly shoved in her pocket, along with the envelope. "Just something I wasn't expecting."

Ellie shrugged but did not seem to be in a hurry to get away. Finally, she said, "I don't think you or your friends had anything to do with my bracelet."

Christie didn't quite know what to say. Thank you for not thinking we ripped you off? Sorry you thought we were crooks? She settled on plain "Thanks," and the two girls went their separate ways. It wasn't until Christie was outside room thirteen that she realized Ellie hadn't said anything about the new girls not being involved in the current thefts!

She opened the door slowly. She hadn't made up her mind about whether to show the note to her roommates or not. She didn't want to involve them or get them upset, but then they were "and Company."

"Hi, get anything interesting?" Vicky was sitting cross-legged on her bed, studying her lines for the play. With her family and friends so close, she communicated by phone.

Maggie picked up on Christie's mood immediately. "What's happened? I know something's wrong."

"So much for a poker face. I may not be cut out for detective work after all. Anyway, this was in my mailbox." She dug the note out of her pocket and flung it in front of Vicky. Maggie sat down next to her.

"This is serious! We've got to tell Terry—or Mrs. Babcox." Two bright red spots appeared on Maggie's cheeks.

"No!" Christie was firm. "It's bad enough the whole school looks at me funny. I don't want all the adults talking about me, too."

Vicky was examining the note carefully. "The words are cut from a magazine, not a newspaper, so we know whoever it is has easier access to *Seventeen,* say, than to the *Boston Globe.* And it's a plain envelope."

Maggie interrupted her. "Ellie's bracelet was returned in a plain envelope, too. I wish there was some way we could compare them."

"And the words are pasted onto three-ring notebook paper—like every student here has." Vicky was examining the letter with the care she normally reserved for "as is" merchandise in one of her favorite bargain spots.

"Well, that does tell us one thing," Christie said.

"What?" Maggie was wearing a sweatshirt displaying a cartoon of a hound in a Sherlock Holmes deerstalker hat. He was smoking a Holmesian pipe and carrying a magnifying glass—the Hound of the Baskervilles from the Conan Doyle story she'd told her roommates. As she spoke, she thought she ought to be able to come up with a question better suited to her outfit; she tried to think deductively.

Christie answered decisively. "That it was probably a student. And someone familiar enough with Widow to know where the mailboxes are."

"So, someone who lives in the dorm or visits a lot." Maggie's mind had slipped into gear.

"Also a neat cutter. Probably heavily into paper dolls when she was little." Vicky was holding the paper close to her face.

"Or one of those compulsively tidy types," Christie added.

"Did you get any other mail?" Maggie asked her.

"Yes, a letter from Hallie. I haven't even had a chance to open it."

"Was the note on top of Hallie's letter or under it?" Maggie was tempted to get her own deerstalker, a Christmas present from her parents, and put it on.

"On top of it. Why? Oh, wait, I know. That means it was put there after the mail delivery on Saturday. And all the eighth graders were on the trip. It had to be somebody from outside Widow! Way to go, Maggie!"

"Unless the person put it in just as we were returning," Vicky said.

"So, we're back to square one." Christie sighed.

Maggie persisted. "I still think it would have been hard for someone to put something in your mailbox with all the hustle and bustle tonight. Whoever it is wouldn't have wanted to be seen, even if it is our beloved Marcia or one of her friends."

"But meanwhile, what do we do?" Maggie was upset. "Anonymous letters are nothing to sneeze at. Christie, you have to take very good care of yourself."

Christie laughed. It was the first funny thing about the whole situation. "I don't intend to get a cold, or germs of any kind," she said solemnly. "Remember, the first swim meet is next Saturday, so I won't be sneezing at anything."

Vicky leaped off the bed and started doing her nightly exercises. Stretching out across her leg, she said, "We have something more important to do than discuss the common cold, fellow detectives. We've got to find out who's taking all this stuff, and I have a feeling that once we do that, we'll also have our poison-pen pal."

Terry called another all-eighth-grade meeting on Monday, this time during the afternoon so the day students could attend. She spoke sternly about the thefts and urged the girls not to leave money or valuables lying about. Since the doors to their rooms didn't lock, because of concern about fire, they could take things to the housemother's suite. It had a large closet that did lock.

Marcia, as class president, made a speech about this sort of thing never happening at Cabot before, and the new girls left the room feeling angry and hurt.

"It's hard to write home," Maggie wailed. "My mother had some kind of perfect *Little Women*–type experience here. I don't know what to say, so I just stick to schoolwork. She's going to know for sure something's wrong. My mom is like the eagle eye of the neighborhood."

Vicky looked puzzled.

Maggie explained. "No matter where we've lived, even in huge New York City, my mom knew every kid in my school, who the parents were, what they did, who was having problems, who wasn't. One time, I heard the mother of one of my friends asking her about something that had happened. My friend was telling her, 'Mom, it was like nothing to get upset about.' And the mother goes, 'Well, I can always call Mrs. Porter!' I thought I would die. So, if I do write, Mom's bound to know something's up, and if I don't, she'll be down here in a flash."

"We'll help you," Vicky assured her. "You're too open. I can think of all sorts of stuff for you to put in. Describe the changing leaves. You want to be a writer. Invent!"

Maggie brightened. This was a challenge.

Christie was barely listening to them. She didn't want to be late for practice. The meet was only a few days away! It was at home, a big advantage, and she was feeling good. Every morning, she had pushed herself to get up and run in the increasingly cold air. Today there had been frost on the ground. Then she went to the pool, did some laps, and practiced her dives. Some divers didn't do laps, but she always had. When she was in the water, Cabot and all her problems melted away.

Today's practice was no different. Christie was focused, and she beamed at the coach's praise. Even the Lloyd sisters' obvious hostility in the locker room couldn't bring her down. She dried her hair and went straight to the dining room, ready to eat a horse. She was laughing to herself as she entered. What a strange phrase!

"You seem really up," Imani said. "Maybe you haven't seen what's for dinner."

The food at Cabot was pretty good, but every once in a while the kitchen inflicted the students with what someone several generations back had termed "mystery meat." That's what it was tonight. Remembering her thoughts as she entered the room, Christie decided to load up on salad, fruit, and rolls.

That's why she was still hungry back in her room a few hours later.

"Who wants popcorn?" she asked her roommates.

Maggie was working on a paper for English class. They were reading Emerson and she'd picked his essay "Self-Reliance" to write about. "Whoso would be a man [Maggie mentally added "or woman"] must be a non-conformist." She liked that. She also liked "To be great is to be misunderstood," and planned to work it into the inevitable argument she'd be having with her parents the next time she was home.

"I'd love some—and I'd love a break," she answered. "I'll help you make it. How about you, Vicky?"

"I have to finish this problem set first. Call me when it's ready, okay?"

The girls had been scrupulous about eating in the common room. The idea of swarms of ants in number thirteen was a powerful deterrent to munching in bed.

Christie and Maggie walked down the quiet hall. As usual, the third-floor common room was empty, even though there were three doubles on the floor besides room thirteen. The only time Christie and Company ran into anyone was in the bathroom. The other girls seemed to prefer their friends on the lower floors to making new acquaintances.

Maggie looked around the empty room. It was furnished with a well-worn couch, a few easy chairs, and a small table with chairs. A framed reproduction of a Degas painting of ballet dancers hung on the wall, which was papered with a pale green stripe, unlike their rooms, which were painted uniformly off-white. She loved this room, tucked under the eaves, with one large hexagonal window looking out over the campus. The glass in the window was wavy and made the whole school look underwater. That reminded her.

"You're not nervous about the meet, are you?" she asked Christie.

"No, not now anyway. I sometimes get wicked nervous the night before. My mom used to make cocoa for me and . . ." The image of her mother, smiling, holding Christie's free hand while she drank the rich, warm chocolaty milk took away her words. It was so real for an instant—as clear as the dancers on the wall—that Christie almost cried out.

"Would it help to talk about her?" Maggie asked gently. "I know she must have been wonderful to have a daughter like you."

Christie shook her head. If she started to talk about her mother, she knew she would fall apart, and that was the last thing she wanted now. Don't think about it. Don't think about it.

Maggie was half-right—Mom was wonderful. Only she didn't have a wonderful daughter. A wonderful daughter didn't wish her father dead. Don't think about it. Don't think about it. She closed her eyes hard until the black behind her lids turned a pulsing red.

Vicky's voice interrupted Christie's thoughts. "I couldn't resist the smell. Math can wait. Let's eat!"

"I see we have the place to ourselves for a change," Vicky continued sarcastically. "There are some advantages to being outcasts. You don't have to share any goodies with the whole floor."

She was about to elaborate when Maggie put her finger to her lips. "Sssh," she whispered. "Do you hear something?"

"Is this more of your fabled imagination?" Christie asked, but then she heard it, too. *Thump, thump, thump.* Heavy footsteps directly overhead!

For a moment, the girls froze. The noise stopped, started again, and stopped. Someone—or something—was creeping about Widow.

Maggie swallowed her popcorn. "We must not be the top floor. There's an attic or a crawl space above us."

"Definitely an attic in a house this old," Christie said. "That must be where those narrow stairs at the landing go."

"Well, what are we waiting for? Come on!" Vicky was on her feet and halfway out of the room.

"With three of us, we have the element of surprise," Maggie pointed out.

Stopping by room thirteen to get their flashlights and take their shoes off, the girls then crept noiselessly up the narrow flight of stairs.

"Dust," mouthed Christie. She was in front. No one had come this way—at least not recently.

The door was almost totally obscured by the thick cobwebs festooned from the ceiling. The air in the old stairwell was so musty, she could taste it, although her mouth was dry with fear. She reached up to brush the webs away and a large spider raced across the beam of her flashlight, casting eerie shadows on the wall. No one had been in the house for fifty years and the gas fixtures on the wall indicated that it may have been even longer. "I've had enough. I'm turning back," a frightened voice to her rear stammered. "Go if you must, but I'm not giving up now. I have to find out what's behind that door!" She heard the footsteps retreating hurriedly down the stairs and kept going. At the top, she trained her light steadily on the large ornate brass doorknob. As she reached for it, it began to turn. Slowly, slowly—turning from the other side!

"Maggie! Come back! The door's open." Christie sounded a little exasperated.

The three girls stepped inside the attic and were somewhat disappointed. Not only wasn't there any unearthly presence or someone imprisoned for years with no hope of escape until they came along; there wasn't much of anything at all. Certainly nothing that could have produced any noise. It was large enough for all the things associated with old attics—steamer trunks, castoffs from bygone eras, dressmaker's dummies—but there were only a few heavy, worn oak desks that must have been the predecessors of the more modern ones in their rooms. There were also some chairs in need of repair and a couple of chests of drawers.

Maggie discovered a light switch, catching it in her beam. She flicked it on and the room was filled with a feeble light from two naked bulbs at either end.

It was also filled with an enormous raccoon, which came lumbering out from behind one of the desks as soon as the lights went on.

"Omigod!" Maggie cried out. "I've never seen one this big. Quick, we have to do something. They can be rabid!"

"Look," Christie said. "There's another door!"

All was not lost.

They ran toward it, keeping their distance from the raccoon, which did not seem any more thrilled at their company than they at its. The door was locked, but the key was in it. Vicky quickly opened it. It led directly to the roof. The widow's walk was a few yards away.

"I don't know how it got in, but let's hope it decides to accept our invitation," Christie said. The three girls held the door open wide, crouching behind it. For what seemed like hours, the raccoon prowled around the attic, upsetting chairs and sniffing at the furniture. The shrill cry of a night bird seemed to remind it of its natural habitat and at last it made its way to the door, quickly slipping into the darkness. The girls closed it hurriedly.

"Phew!" Maggie breathed a sigh of relief. "All I could think of was having to have those shots. The needles are supposed to be a foot long or something."

"This is one of the few times I'm glad I don't have your colorful imagination," Vicky commented. "Now, how do you suppose it got in?"

It wasn't hard to figure out. There was a louvered section that had fallen out from the bottom of an open window overlooking the roof.

"Do you think it's gone?" Christie asked.

"Probably," Maggie said. "It was obviously searching for food and I'll bet it's out by the trash cans now."

"Good. I want to see what's in the widow's walk."

The girls opened the door cautiously and walked out onto the flat roof.

"So that's why the roofline of the house has such an odd look," Maggie observed. "I noticed it the first day.

It seems to stop and then dip down to the widow's walk. It, or this attic story, must have been added later.''

"I'll bet the attic is where they slept in the olden days when there weren't so many dormitories. You know, good for those Victorian maidens to sleep in a garret.''

"It's beautiful up here. You can see the whole campus, and when the leaves are off the trees, we'll probably be able to look right straight into Aleford center,'' Maggie enthused.

"Yeah, that teeming metropolis.'' Vicky had found it hard to believe that the only clothing store Aleford boasted was for ladies of a certain size and age. It had been there forever, as had virtually everything else in Aleford, and was called La Mode Dress Shoppe.

Christie was crossing the roof and walking around the glassed-in widow's walk, shining her flashlight at the structure. "There has to be an opening. What did the poor woman do in bad weather?''

Vicky joined her. "There is. You can see it better from farther away. One of the windows is hinged, so it must be a door.''

It was, but the layer of dead flies and one dead bat that greeted them upon opening it caused them to hastily slam it shut. They walked back to the attic, shivering in the chilly night air.

"Our ghostly presence—a raccoon.'' Maggie laughed.

"One case solved,'' Vicky said. "Shall we finish our popcorn and think about the other?''

"By all means. The popcorn, that is. But I'm too tired to think—elementary though it may be, Watson. Tomorrow let's make a list, the way they do in proper mystery books, then see what we've got,'' Christie said.

They closed the door to the outside, locked it, then replaced the louvered window section.

"We should tell Terry. We don't want any more nocturnal intruders, and someone should nail this in tighter," Vicky suggested. They turned off the lights and went back to the common room.

"The widow's walk must be just above our room," Maggie said reflectively. Then, seeing the wide-eyed look on Christie's face, she stopped and changed the subject to what they might read to the nursing-home patients. Maybe the idea of sleeping just below a dead bat and goodness knows how many lifeless flies was not one Christie wanted to think about just before she got into bed.

Wednesday, a computer was taken, a laptop belonging to one of the girls on the third floor. Christie and Company were resigned to the looks sent their way by now, but the whole thing was definitely getting out of hand.

"Who could be doing this!" Vicky exploded. "It can't be a kleptomaniac. I've always heard they take things without regard to what they're worth, and whoever is taking these things knows what's valuable—and salable."

Christie nodded her head in agreement. "There was a girl like that in my old school. Every once in a while, we'd get her to empty her backpack and recover whatever we were missing. She had a definite fondness for Walkmans, but you're right—she also took chewed-up old pencils, barrettes, paper clips."

"Like a magpie—you know, as in the bird," Maggie said. "Shiny objects. You can find anything from a diamond ring to a piece of aluminum foil in their nests."

"This isn't getting us anywhere," Vicky complained. "We have to start thinking logically—means, motive, opportunity, that stuff."

"Can we do it after Saturday? I really have to get to practice now and I want to focus on the meet and not think about anything else," Christie asked.

"Sure, a few days more or less won't matter."

There were no more thefts Thursday and Friday, but the eighth grade was still jumpy. Terry had had requests to lock up everything from a pair of diamond studs to a well-worn teddy bear.

Friday night, Maggie disappeared after she put her beloved Latin away. She wished she felt so confident about all her subjects. As she left, she told her roommates to meet her in their common room at nine.

"I wonder what's up?" Vicky asked.

"I have no idea," Christie said. "I can't concentrate. Want me to hear your lines?"

"That would be great. I'm really getting into this part. It's frightening, though, when you think that all those innocent people were hanged as witches in Salem, falsely accused, and all because of a group of hysterical teenaged girls."

Frightening was not the word for it, Christie thought. She knew the story of the play and how the girls had worked themselves into fits, eventually turning against one another out of fear. She listened to Vicky's lines. She was good and didn't overact. Christie could almost believe that timid, easily influenced Mary Warren was sitting next to her, not Victoria Lee, her opinionated, strong-minded roommate.

At nine, they went down the hall to the common

room. Maggie was sitting at the table. A steaming mug of hot cocoa was set at each place and a plate of cookies in the middle.

"I hope it's the way you like it." She looked up anxiously at Christie—the words *the way your mother made it* unspoken.

Christie threw her arms around Maggie. "It's perfect. You're so terrific to do this. I just know tomorrow is going to be out of this world."

❖ Chapter Seven

LOOKING BACK ON THE EVENTS OF THAT
Saturday morning, Christie remembered her words of
the night before. The day *had* been out of this world.
What she hadn't realized was that the world would be
one so far away and bizarre—say like Mars.

It started as soon as she entered the gym. She opened
her locker and found a familiar white envelope staring up
at her from the bottom, resting on top of the spare running
shoes she kept there. Another one of those notes! She
reached for it, then drew back. Someone was trying to
psych her out before the meet, and she wasn't about to
give her, or him, the pleasure of watching it work. The
message was bound to be the same. Whatever it was, she
resolved to forget the whole thing for now and concentrate
only on good hurdles—the jump to the end of the board—
and rip entries—hands together, head straight.

She gave herself a little pep talk. You feel great.
You've been training for months. Visions of sit-ups,
pike stretches, and endless "stairs"—running up and
down the bleachers—floated across her mind. Nothing
is going to spoil this meet!

Her good intentions got her through changing, and it wasn't until she was doing her warm-up exercises that the nagging thoughts—and fears—at the back of her mind began to creep forward. Why was this happening to her? Guiltily, she wondered why Vicky and Maggie weren't being included. They were all new. And they were all in room thirteen.

Coach Stevens was talking to the whole team in the locker room.

"I know you'll go out there and do your best. I don't expect anything less. It's our first meet, but it's theirs, too. Always remember, the competition is just as nerved up as you are." She smiled at the group's solemn faces. "Now, have some fun. You've been working hard and you look good—maybe even better than good." She motioned them out the door and there was a bit of a jam as the entire team squeezed through.

That's when the second thing happened. Christie tripped, or was tripped. All of a sudden, she found herself on the hard, cold locker room floor. She'd broken the fall with her hand and her wrist was already throbbing.

Coach Erica Stevens was at her side immediately. "Christie, are you okay?" she asked anxiously.

"I think so. My wrist is a little sore," Christie answered slowly, and got to her feet.

"Let me get a cold pack. Fortunately, you have some time before your event. You do feel well enough to dive, don't you? Not dizzy, anything like that?"

"I feel fine, except for my wrist. I didn't hit my head."

Several of the girls said, "Tough luck," commiserating, but Christie could feel tension coming from somewhere. She just couldn't put her finger on it—or rather, her.

Sitting by the side of the pool nursing her wrist, Christie forced herself to relax, enjoying the familiar smell of chlorine and the warm, damp air.

The schools exchanged cheers, shook hands, and squared off for the competition. There was a small audience on the bleachers. Christie wasn't expecting anyone. There were some parents, but she knew hers wouldn't be there. Mom had come to all her meets, even some practices, until she got too sick. Christie pushed that thought to the rear of her mind, too. It was getting pretty crowded back there.

Then she saw her roommates. Vicky gave a big wave and Maggie a thumbs-up sign. Marine, who was Christie's Cabot Guide, was with them, grinning broadly. It was like magic. Christie's wrist stopped hurting, or at least she stopped being aware of it, and all that mattered was the meet. She began to go over the dives in her head. Visualization—the coach's favorite technique.

Cabot was doing well. The other school had a strong team, but event after event went to the blue-and-gold suits.

It was time for the diving competition. Eight dives. Five requireds and three optionals. Eight dives from a three-meter springboard and it would all be over. Over too fast. Christie felt the rush of adrenaline that competitions always brought. She was pumped up and ready. Her first dive went well. Not brilliant, but nothing to knock her out of the running. She went back to her place and reached for her "Sammy," the small square of absorbent cloth each diver used to dry off between dives. Jessica Lloyd had just finished what looked to

Christie like a perfect front dive pike. The girl was Olympic material, she thought admiringly.

Christie brought the cloth up to her face and stopped suddenly. It smelled funny, like vinegar or some chemical. She dropped it to the ground. Someone had tampered with it—or switched cloths! What would have happened if she had rubbed her arms and legs first! Her palms already felt prickly. What was she going to do? She went to the coach and told her she was going to the bathroom. Erica Stevens was preoccupied with the event. "Okay, okay, but hurry up. It's almost time for your second dive."

As she went into the locker room to wash her hands, Christie began to get mad. Notes, trying to mess her up in the meet. Who hated her this much? Marcia? One of her friends? She scrubbed her hands with soap until they were pink. She couldn't feel any itching anymore and assumed whatever it was had washed off. Should she tell the coach? Her dive! She raced back to the pool.

No, she wouldn't tell Coach Stevens. But she would tell "and Company."

The Cabot divers continued to do well and it was obvious that they would win the event. Christie felt proud of her teammates. She had only one dive left, an optional and a difficult one: an inward two and a half. She'd practiced it so often, she felt as if she could do it on dry land. She took her first step, then her second, eyes fixed on the end of the board, ready to get the height she needed.

A shot rang out! A few people let out inadvertent cries of surprise.

It wasn't a shot, of course. Someone had dropped a

book from the bleachers, and when it hit the concrete floor, the noise reverberated throughout the room.

Startled, Christie's foot came down hard. She swayed to one side, recovered, and went for it.

Vicky and Maggie turned angrily in the direction of the noise, but they didn't see anyone they knew.

"Somebody did that on purpose! Somebody was deliberately trying to destroy her concentration! And I'm going to find out who!" Vicky fumed.

"But it didn't work. Look!" Maggie said.

It was a beautiful dive. The judges thought so, too, and awarded her an 8.0, the highest mark of the day. The place burst into applause and Christie was surrounded by her teammates. The coach gave her a big hug.

But someone among her well-wishers was out to get her.

Exhilarated, Christie met Vicky, Maggie, and Marine outside the gym. The diving part of the meet was finished and she was free for the rest of the day.

The girls all started talking at once. Congratulations— and speculations about who had dropped the book.

"I'm sure it was an accident," Marine reassured Christie. "No one would do such a thing on purpose! It was wonderful to watch you, but now"—she gave a heavy sigh—"it's all day in the library for me. *Au revoir!*"

Christie was touched that Marine had come. She watched her disappear from sight and then thought about the morning. Before she'd left the pool, she'd gone back to where she'd left her Sammy and, with her back to the group remaining, had picked it up gingerly with a wad of paper towels. She'd wrapped it in a thick layer and dropped it in the bottom of her locker, planning to return with a plastic bag. Maybe they'd be able to figure out what was on it. She'd also put the unopened letter into her knapsack. There was no way she wanted to read it yet. All she wanted to do for the next few hours was celebrate. The three roommates had been given permission to go into Boston.

Vicky had every minute planned. They'd head straight for Filene's Basement, then take the MBTA out to Brookline and have supper at the the Ginger Jar. Her father had agreed to drive them back to school.

"You were fantastic!" Maggie exclaimed. "I would never have been able to stay so calm after that doofus dropped a book."

Christie hadn't intended to tell them, but somehow as they walked toward the bus, she found herself relating the events of what she knew she'd always regard as the meet from hell—even though things did turn out all right. Now that it was over, she was aware that her wrist still hurt.

"Did you feel someone pushing you?" Vicky asked.

"Everyone was pushing a little. We all wanted to get to the pool. But it wasn't a push. It felt more like a foot shoved between my legs as I was moving forward."

"We have to find someone who's taking chemistry, a junior or senior, and get them to analyze your towel thingy, whatever it's called," Maggie suggested.

"Maybe Mark could do it. Even though he's in tenth grade, he's some kind of science genius, and I heard him say he was taking chemistry this year."

"That would be great, especially for you," Christie teased Vicky. "You could be like one of those husband-

and-wife teams who discover all sorts of things for the benefit of humankind—you know, like the Curies.''

"Very funny. I like the boy. He's a great actor. We're in a play together. I'm *not* planning to marry him.''

In the end, they had to run for the bus. When they finally emerged on Washington Street at Downtown Crossing in the center of Boston, the afternoon was getting shorter and shorter.

"This will just give you a taste of Filene's Basement. You really need a whole day,'' Vicky explained as they descended several flights of stairs beneath the main department store.

Maggie looked around. While not the madhouse she had been led to expect from some descriptions—customers coming to blows over a bargain, others snatching desired articles of clothing when someone was struggling modestly to try something on—it was still pretty chaotic. There was a small women's dressing room now, but the line was so long that most people did as they had always done, achieving acrobatic wonders as one dress or blouse went on beneath another, the top one removed, and then the whole process reversed.

"I usually wear a leotard,'' Vicky told them, "but today I didn't bother since I'm looking for a sweater.''

Christie was excited. "I can't believe I live so close and never came here. You can get anything!''

Vicky nodded. "They even have a travel agency. One of my cousins got all the stuff for her wedding here but the food and the band—their rings, the honeymoon tickets, and her dress. Once a year, they have a huge sale on wedding dresses, gowns that cost thousands for a fraction of the price. You think it's nuts today, you should have been here then. Her mother, her sister, my mother, me, and a few more cousins all came with her to grab gowns, no matter what size to trade for the ones we wanted. We'd guard the pile while she went off to see what other people had. It was great, and she got a gorgeous dress.'' Vicky remembered how much fun that day had been. Even her mother had joined in, swept away by their contagious enthusiasm. At lunch in Chinatown afterward, they couldn't stop laughing. Vicky had thought it might lead to greater closeness with her mother, but the next day everything was the same. Business as usual. She sighed.

''What is it?'' Maggie asked. Out of the three, she was the quickest to pick up on her roommates' changes of mood.

''I was thinking about my mother. We used to be close, but somehow we just can't talk to each other anymore.''

''Have you tried telling her how you feel?'' Maggie asked.

''No, I'm afraid of what she might say. I guess I assume she'd just deny the whole thing and I'd be back where I started, except totally humiliated.''

Listening to them talk, Christie wondered how she and her mother would be getting along now. She knew lots of girls who fought with their mothers—and lots who didn't. Maggie talked about her mother as a kind of dragon, but there was strong affection underneath it all. Until her mom got sick, Christie told her everything, and she still remembered her mother's wise words when a friendship had turned out not to be what Christie had expected, as well as that famous time in third grade when she had spelled the word *bowl* as *bowel*—in front of the whole class. She had never wanted to go back to school again, but her mother told her such funny stories of similar embarrassments when she had been young that Christie forgot her own.

"Where do you want to start?" Vicky asked.

"We're here to watch a pro at work, so look for your sweater and we'll follow humbly in your footsteps," Maggie suggested.

For the next hour, they looked at sweaters on both floors and in all sorts of departments, even men's. Vicky finally settled on a black hand-knit cardigan with huge cables and Cracker Jack charms for buttons.

"Filene's Basement has this automatic markdown policy. If it doesn't sell after such and such a date, they mark it down, and again and again. Then if it's still around, it goes to charity. This is a good buy even with just the first markdown. I absolutely loved that cashmere DKNY, but it was way, way, way over my budget."

Maggie had found a striped turtleneck that met with Vicky's approval, teal blue and purple. It was only eight dollars.

"I know why you love this place so much," Christie said. The girls were looking at a rack of elaborately beaded evening gowns—FROM A FAMOUS NEW YORK STORE, the sign read. "It's kind of an adult version of playing dress-up. Imagine wearing these things!"

"Exactly," Vicky replied. "Now you have to get something, too. Maybe not this number." She pulled out a slinky black satin full-length gown with long, tight lace sleeves. "At least not yet. How about a tie? It would look cool with those big painter's overalls you have."

"I never thought of dressing like my father. A tie!"

"Come on, at least look."

99

They went over to a wall covered with rows and rows of ties—expensive silks, cheap synthetics—in one grand mishmash. They started searching. Christie laughed. "How about this?" It was a sedate paisley tie—with Sylvester and Tweetie Bird superimposed over the swirls.

"Perfect! And only—"

Maggie grabbed Vicky's arm and pulled her into the next aisle. "Get over here quick! Come on, Christie!"

The two looked at her in bewilderment, which heightened as she crouched down behind a rack of trousers.

"It's Mr. Pritchard," she whispered. "And he's with some woman."

Christie peeked through the folds of material. The wool felt scratchy. She hoped they were lined. Maggie was right. It was the English teacher—and he was with *some* woman!

The woman was dressed in a short, tight red sheath. Her high heels sent her towering above Pritchard's Adam's apple. She had long dark hair, artfully arranged in loose curls. Her lipstick and nail polish matched the dress. At the moment, she was picking out several ties. The girls couldn't quite make out the conversation, but from the way she was holding them up to him, it was apparent she was selecting appropriate neckwear for the Cabot faculty member and not someone else. She seemed confident in her selection. He grimaced at one, but she shook her head and didn't put it back on the rack.

"They ought to be looking at ascots," Maggie whispered, "or high turtlenecks."

"Stop it," Vicky said. "You're going to make me laugh."

"He doesn't really know us," Christie said. "None

of us have him. Why doesn't someone try to get a little closer and we'll meet over by that counter we passed with all the dishes and picture frames? What did you call it, Vicky? Giftware? Three girls hiding behind a rack of men's pants is going to start to look a little odd, even in Filene's Basement."

"It was your idea, you go," Maggie said.

They split up and Christie nonchalantly walked over as close as she dared, keeping her face to the wall and scrutinizing the ties. Maybe she should get one for her father for Christmas.

"Blue brings out the color of your eyes. I like the blue one," the woman said.

"I don't see why I need to have so many!" Mr. Pritchard protested.

"Don't be silly. We can't have you turning into one of those schoolteachers with the ragged shirt cuffs and baggy trousers."

Christie recalled the hole in Mr. Pritchard's sock. The threat was real. She snuck a long look at the woman and was even more surprised. She was young, early twenties tops. Oh, Mr. Pritchard!

The two moved off with their purchases to the register and Christie followed with her Tweetie Bird tie. Boldly, she stood in line behind them.

"What next, my dear?"

"Jewelry," the woman said firmly.

"Then jewelry it is."

Christie suppressed a shocked gasp with difficulty and waited impatiently as they paid the salesclerk.

In the giftware department, Maggie and Vicky were looking at baskets.

"You can't make one on a machine, you know,"

Maggie said. "Every one is woven by somebody in some part of the world." When she had heard this, it had astonished her and she kept imagining who might have labored over each new one her mother brought home. She told Vicky, "My mother has hundreds of them around the inn, filled with dried flowers, magazines, whatever. Maybe I'll come back and get one of these for her for Christmas."

"If you see something you really want and the price is right, you have to get it right away," Vicky advised. "Everything's constantly changing. That's why it's so great."

"It's a good thing you're out in Aleford. I think you're dangerously close to Basement dependency," Maggie teased her friend.

Meanwhile, Christie was expertly keeping her quarry in sight, ducking behind racks of clothing when they stopped to browse and resuming her surveillance as they moved on. The woman had her arm casually linked through Mr. Pritchard's. There was one tense moment when the pair suddenly turned around, coming face-to-face with Christie. Mr. Pritchard frowned slightly and Christie fully expected him to confront her, but instead he said, "I think those blouses were on another rack, sweetheart." Christie let them get far ahead, but not away, before picking up the trail again, which did indeed end at the fine-jewelry counter.

She retraced her steps back to giftware. Her roommates both spied Christie at the same moment and went running over to her.

"You'll never guess!" she told them. "They're at the jewelry counter now! She's really young—around Terry's age."

"Old Pritchard. What could she see in him?" Maggie wondered.

"It might be pretty expensive to have a young, beautiful girlfriend." Vicky was speculating out loud. "Don't you remember we saw Mr. Pritchard coming out of Widow as we were going to breakfast before the trip last Saturday? The knapsacks were still in the study. And he certainly could have been in the dorm at other times. No one would ever think to suspect a teacher."

"I can't believe it!" Maggie was astounded. She'd never thought of her teachers as really having lives outside the classroom, which was silly, but somehow their world seemed all contained in what they did there.

Christie seemed to think Vicky's idea wasn't too crazy. "Somebody needs to stay on the trail. You go this time, Vicky. They saw me, and it might look suspicious if I turn up again. Besides, you know about jewelry. See if you can find out how much what they're looking at costs. We'll stay put right here."

The huge diamond caught the light and sent it dancing about the room in a myriad of tiny rainbows. Her long, elegant fingers, each crowned with a perfect pink shell of a nail, were made for a ring like this. "Like it?" he asked. "I adore it, but . . ." She fell silent. "But what? Tell me. The setting can be changed, anything. Oh, give it back to me now. I should have known. It is not good enough for you."

"Oh no! It's perfect! It's the most exquisite jewel I've ever seen, but I cannot accept such a gift. I could never wear it without thinking what its cost could mean to the children. You know I have devoted my life to helping them. Until a cure is found for poverty, there can be no other choice."

"Where are you now?" Christie's amused voice broke in and Maggie was slightly surprised to find herself looking at a shelf filled with electric bun warmers and not on the streets of a far-away city.

She blushed. Her day—and night—dreams were only revealed in her journal.

"No place special. What do you think could be keeping Vicky? Maybe she's following them someplace else. Didn't you say this place sold furs?"

"Yes! Wow, this is really getting interesting. Just goes to show, you can't judge a book by its cover."

Vicky returned. Her eyes were sparkling. "They really have some great stuff."

"But what about Mr. Pritchard? What was *he* looking at?"

"Earrings, but they were gold and expensive, even for here. She was making all the decisions, like with the ties. I'd say she pretty much has him on a leash."

"Woof, woof." Maggie's mental image of the schoolmaster on a lead was a vivid one.

"But not diamonds or rubies—nothing he'd have to mortgage his house for, if he has one."

"Or pilfer from students," Christie added.

"Not for today's purchases, anyway. Then they left the store. I followed them out to Washington Street. It looked as if they were headed into that big bookstore down the block."

"Well, the man *is* an English teacher."

"True. Now, we have to get going ourselves if we want to have time to eat before my dad takes us back. We can get on the subway from down here."

"You're right," Maggie said. "This place is perfect."

104

On the subway, Christie remembered the letter still unopened in her backpack. It had been such a great day. She was really happy with her performance at the meet; then the trip to Filene's Basement had been exciting and fun in a way she never would have predicted. It was a long ride out to Brookline and the train made frequent stops. At each one, she said to herself, I'll open it by the next stop. It was beginning to obsess her. Finally, she unzipped the bag and tore open the envelope. Her roommates were on either side. Neither had wanted to press Christie into opening the envelope, although ever since hearing about it, Maggie, for one, had been filled with curiosity. Would it be the same message?

It wasn't. Same method, same crudeness—only this one was worse.

A woMa**n** wIt**H** Ca**N**cer ShoUldn't HAv**e** a B**o**BY. I**t** cAn **KilL** HeR.

❖ Chapter Eight

"**C**HRISTIE! CHRISTIE!" MAGGIE FLUNG AN arm around her friend's shoulder, trying to get her attention. As soon as Christie had read the words, she'd tumbled into some sort of hole, seeing and hearing nothing. Her face had lost all its color and her friends were seriously worried. It had lasted only a few seconds, but it felt like a year.

"I'm okay," she said slowly.

"No, you're not," Vicky declared. She and Maggie had read along with Christie. "And we're not. Nothing or nobody's going to be normal again until we find the creep—or creeps—behind this."

"I can't believe someone would stoop so low. A total and complete lie. You know that, don't you? Getting pregnant can't give you cancer. You've got to talk to us, Christie. Please," Maggie implored. "You can't let them get to you. There's no way having you made your mom sick. I'll bet it was just the opposite."

Christie nodded. It was true her mother used to say that the best day of her life was when she discovered she was pregnant and that Christie was the best thing that had ever happened to her parents. But it was also true that Christie had seen an article in a magazine just before her mother died. She remembered it vividly. She was in the waiting room at the hospital. Her mother was in X ray or someplace like that, someplace her daughter couldn't go. Christie had idly picked up the magazine and the headline on the article jumped out at her: LINK BETWEEN PREGNANCY AND BREAST CANCER? She had read it, unable to stop herself. The article was way too complicated, but Christie had understood that one of its points was that the change in a woman's hormones during pregnancy could cause the cancer cells to grow.

She shook her head. This whole thing was getting to be too much for her. The only people she had told about her mother dying of cancer were Maggie and Vicky. Mrs. Babcox probably knew, and that meant Terry, too. But they hadn't said anything to her—thank goodness. One of the worst things about her mom's death had been sympathy from well-meaning adults. Christie had wanted to scream at them, It wasn't *your* mother!

"How did the person know?" Christie spoke her question out loud. Her roommates exchanged uncomfortable glances. Then Vicky looked straight at Christie. "Maggie and I assumed you wanted to keep your mother's death private. We never mentioned it to anyone, but Imani asked us about it at the beginning of school. It seems Terry told some of the girls. Imani wanted to know if she could do anything to help, talk to you, you know."

Christie's cheeks burned. So everybody knew.

Vicky was tugging at her. "Come on, this is our stop."

They walked to the restaurant in the twilight and suddenly Christie found herself confiding in her friends about her mother for the first time. She told them about the magazine article.

"Did you ever talk to your dad about the article?"

Christie shook her head. She'd said enough. There was no way she was going to get into the whole thing about her father now.

"I think you need to find out the truth—from a doctor or someone else who can really give you the answers. Whoever wrote that note probably saw the same article somewhere," Maggie said emphatically. "The most important thing is that you were born long before your mother got sick, right?"

Christie nodded. "I think so, but what if—"

"No 'what ifs.' We'll get the facts. We're detectives, aren't we?"

Maggie's determination was producing results and Christie permitted herself a small smile.

"What I don't get is why Christie? Why not us, too? We're all in this together. You got some cocoa spilled on you and a rubber snake in your sleeping bag, but that's almost to be expected—the kind of stuff that happens to new kids. Nothing like what's happening to Christie." Vicky was thinking out loud. "And no one has done anything particular to me, except give me the cold shoulder."

"Quick, knock on wood," Christie said, only half in jest.

Vicky touched a tree trunk in passing and smiled. They were almost to the restaurant. She was hungry, and what's more, she was sure that the Ginger Jar would take Christie's mind off the letter.

"Come on, let's hurry. I want some pot stickers!"

108

*   *   *

The Lees greeted all three girls as if they had not seen them for several years, rather than several weeks. There were only a few early diners and the Lees had time to sit with them and drink some hot, fragrant jasmine tea. Old Mrs. Lee, who had not been at the picnic, was introduced and immediately pulled her granddaughter aside for a private chat. Vicky raised her eyebrows at her friends, but she was delighted to see her grandmother again. She wished she could tell her everything that had happened and magically have this wise woman tell her what to do, but Vicky knew that the result would be worry and upset—for the whole family.

Her father was calling to her. "Pot stickers, daughter. You can tell me what else you want to eat, but I know you want these."

Even Vicky's mother was smiling. "Some restaurants call these 'Peking ravioli,' " she told Christie and Maggie, who were eagerly consuming the crescent-shaped dumplings that were filled with ground meat, scallions, and ginger, then steamed.

"We used to eat them in Chinatown all the time when I lived in New York City," Maggie told them. "I haven't had such good pot stickers since then. Maine does better with chowder and blueberry pie."

Both girls looked around the restaurant in appreciation. The Lees had decorated the interior in many shades of red and gold—red for good luck. Their collection of Chinese porcelain was displayed on shelves and in special niches throughout the two large adjoining rooms. Plants and flower arrangements brought a feeling of spring inside, even on the most bitterly cold winter day. At the front of the restaurant stood an enormous blue-

and-white porcelain ginger jar. Vicky used to imagine hiding inside it when she was a little girl. A picture of the jar was on the cover of each menu.

"This is a beautiful room," Christie told the Lees.

Vicky's father beamed at his wife. "Mrs. Lee is responsible for all the decoration and arranges the flowers herself."

"Wow," Maggie said. "You should go into business. It's really hard to design something like this. My mother finally gave up and hired a decorator to help her at the inn. And these flowers! I'd love to watch you sometime."

"It would be my pleasure." Mrs. Lee was genuinely pleased—and embarrassed.

Vicky realized that she took her mother's gifts for granted. Their apartment had also been decorated by her mother, and people commented all the time on how stunning it was, yet inviting. The restaurant was the same. You didn't worry that you'd break something. The brocade on the seats of the chairs wasn't covered in plastic. Mrs. Lee had arranged the porcelains so no one could accidentally knock into them, and she had searched until she found durable and attractive coverings for the chairs. Vicky wondered if some of her mother's ability might have rubbed off on her. She had the feeling she'd be good at choosing colors, putting a room together. Although right now she was concentrating on decorating herself. Maybe her mother had been that way when she was her age. She wished she felt close enough to ask her. She watched the way her mother was talking to her friends. There was a smile on her face and she was responding to their questions about the restaurant in an easy and relaxed manner. When Vicky talked with her, it was the opposite. She was either impatient and her words came tumbling out abruptly or few came at all—just a short, serious, well-considered sentence. Vicky frowned. She didn't want to think about this now. She made herself concentrate on the pot stickers her father had so lovingly offered.

By the time the hungry girls had eaten their way through sizzling rice soup, braised duck with vegetables, shrimp chow fun—a wide rice noodle—and deep-fried, stuffed bean curd, Cabot and the mysterious events there seemed far away.

"How about some moo shi—pork, chicken, or beef?" Mr. Lee suggested.

Vicky groaned. "I wish I had another stomach, Dad." Turning to her roommates, she explained, "Moo shi is delicious. You roll the filling—shredded cabbage, meat, other goodies—up in these thin pancakes. But I can't eat another thing."

"It was all fantastic," Christie said. "We'll have the moo shi next time, and I hope next time is soon."

"Well, at least some litchi nuts and orange sections," Vicky's father offered. "And your fortune cookies. The meal would not be complete without them."

"Make sure the fortunes are good ones," Vicky directed, almost adding before she stopped herself, we can use them.

"All fortunes in fortune cookies are good," said a voice behind her. "The restaurant owners want people to come back. If you got a cookie saying you were going to lose all your money tomorrow or your hair would fall out by summer, you'd never darken the doorway again. And you'd tell all your friends!"

Vicky jumped up and threw her arms around the young Oriental man who had provided this analysis.

"Teddy, I didn't know you would be here!" She turned to her roommates. "This is my cousin Teddy."

"Her favorite cousin, Teddy," he amended, adding, "Didn't Uncle Henry tell you? I'm being trusted to drive you back to that girls' reformatory or wherever they've stuck you, because he had some Chamber of Commerce thing that came up."

"We called the school, and your headmistress said it was fine," Mr. Lee assured the girls.

"You'd think we were made of glass," Maggie protested. "Of course it's fine."

Teddy laughed. "I'm going into the kitchen to get some grub and tease Aunt Virginia. Then we'll get going."

"A hot date?" Vicky didn't like being shortchanged. She had hoped to stop for ice cream once they got back to Aleford. Teddy, a college sophomore, *was* her favorite cousin and she didn't see him often enough.

"No, not tonight anyway, but I have to study. Now, enjoy your fortunes."

The girls each reached for a cookie.

"He seems really cool," Christie said to Vicky, "and very cute. I like his jacket."

Vicky had liked it, too—a dark green woolen baseball jacket with brown leather sleeves. It would look great with a plaid flannel dress she had for winter. She was debating her chances of borrowing it when Maggie read her fortune out loud: " 'Unexpected romantic and financial gifts surprise and delight you!' Well, that's certainly true. Not that I've had much experience," she added as her roommates giggled. "What do yours say?"

" 'Adventure can be real happiness,' " Vicky read. "But lately you have had too much of it."

"You made that up!" Christie cried.

"Not the first part. What does yours say?"

" 'It's a good thing that life is not as serious as it seems to the waiter.' " The three burst into laughter, tears running down their cheeks. It was a release from the tension of the day.

"Now read what it really says," Maggie told her.

"But that is what it really says. Look for yourself," Christie protested, and they started laughing again. The Lees came out of the kitchen to see what the cause of the merriment was.

"Where are you getting your cookies these days?" Vicky asked her father. "Some of the fortunes are like *Saturday Night Live.*"

"Same place as always. Let me see." He chuckled as he read Christie's fortune. "I was your waiter tonight and can assure you that this fortune is one hundred percent accurate."

Teddy came out of the kitchen. "Come on, ladies, your limo—or rather, gently used Chevy—awaits." He hugged his aunt, grandmother, and solemnly shook hands with his uncle. "Don't worry about a thing. All those rumors about my reckless driving are completely false."

Mr. Lee replied, "I know that, Teddy—and they'd better stay that way."

"Dad's only half-kidding," Vicky whispered to Maggie.

"Mine wouldn't be kidding at all," Maggie whispered back. "Parents!"

Vicky was able to persuade Teddy to stop for ice cream without too much trouble. "We'll go to Steve's and you can have Cookeo," she'd told him, telling her friends, "Teddy will eat anything with Oreo cookies crumbled on top."

"Remember when you gave me those noodles with Oreos and I ate them, much to your surprise?"

"And disgust." She made a face. "It was totally gross."

Over ice cream, they laughed some more. Maggie told them the story of how she and her friend Charlene, plus some other kids who rode the school bus to the Little Bittern ferry, got worried when they saw somebody's mother who was waiting behind the wheel of her car for their arrival apparently start to have a fit. They convinced the bus driver to go investigate before they got off, fearing the worst. The driver came back grinning. "She's listening to some music and keeping time!"

"Honestly, we thought she was gone. We couldn't believe she was dancing in the car!" Maggie gave an imitation.

Finally, as their ice cream melted away, they told Teddy some of what had been happening. He took it very seriously.

"I think you should definitely tell the headmistress. These letters sound dangerous. In any case, scapegoating of new kids should be stopped. You know it's somebody who's jealous of you guys. You have more talent, brains, and beauty in each of your pinkie fingers than the sicko who's doing this has in her whole body."

But Christie was adamant. "I don't want Mrs. Babcox to know. We can handle this."

She knew the first thing that would happen was that her father would be called and the adults at school would be all over the three roommates. They'd end up being scapegoated even more for tattling. Besides, she had a plan that she wasn't even sure she was going to tell "and Company" about yet.

"I agree with Christie," Vicky said. "And don't say we're little girls who can't take care of ourselves. We're a lot more likely to find out who's doing this than any of the teachers or Mrs. Babcox."

"What about telling your housemother?" Teddy asked.

Maggie answered for the group. " 'House sister' is more like it. She's okay, but she's very young and only here until they find a permanent replacement." They filled him in on the runaway previous housemother, then gently but firmly moved away from the topic.

"I know you don't want to talk about this anymore," he said to them, taking out a small pad of paper and a pen, "but I want each of you to carry my phone number around and call if you need any kind of help."

"How about doing my homework for me?" Vicky asked.

The next week was as close to normal as a week at Cabot could be, the girls decided the following Friday night. Christie had continued her training regimen, Maggie got an *A* on her first English paper, and Vicky finished memorizing her lines for *The Crucible*. There were no more notes—and no more thefts. But this time, unlike Ellie's bracelet, nothing that had been stolen was returned.

They were in the third-floor common room, waiting for their guides, whom they'd invited up for cocoa and cookies. Marine, Aisha, and Imani continued to be their closest friends.

"We never made the list the way we said we would. You know, who was where when—motive, means, opportunity, that kind of thing," Maggie said. She was in sweats, also wearing her checkered Sherlock Holmes hat. She'd been wearing it often lately—for inspiration, she'd told Vicky, who had questioned its all-too-frequent appearance as a fashion accessory.

"True," Vicky agreed. "Christie and Company has been getting lazy. Let's start while we're waiting."

Maggie produced a small notebook from her pocket. She had dozens of them. "Let's see . . . the only definite suspect we have for the thefts is Mr. Pritchard, who we saw coming out of the dorm the day we went to Cape Cod. Possible motive: expensive girlfriend. But the knapsacks were there the night before, too. Anyone in the dorm could have crept down."

"Which leads us to Marcia, Tina, and that group," Vicky said. "Maybe one of them took Ellie's bracelet knowing it was hers and that's why it was returned once we got accused. I still think these girls are the most likely suspects. They obviously resented our coming into the class, especially Christie, who's major diving competition for Marcia."

"It does make sense," Christie admitted. "And their room is on the first floor. It would be really easy to get to the study—and the mailboxes. I can't see any reason for Mr. Pritchard to be sending me these letters. Plus, Marcia certainly knows where my locker is at the pool." She turned toward Vicky. "When is your friend going to tell you what was on my Sammy?"

Maggie laughed. "It always sounds so funny when you say that."

Christie had given the towel to Vicky earlier in the week, putting it into a plastic bag. At the next rehearsal, Vicky had approached Mark Reese and asked him to analyze it, no questions asked. He had been puzzled, but said he'd give it a try.

"I thought he would have called by now," Vicky said. "At Wednesday's rehearsal, he said he hadn't had a chance to get to it but that he would by this weekend. Maybe I should call him."

"Call who?" It was Aisha. "Come on, no secrets from your guides. Maybe we can give you some tips."

"Mark Reese. He's in the play with Vicky," Christie answered quickly. She trusted their guides, but she didn't want any more people to know what had been happening. In some weird way, she felt responsible, even though she knew that was crazy.

"Mark Reese! Hello! We *are* aiming high—an older man. Good luck!" Imani teased Vicky. "He'd be a nice one to bring home to Mom and Dad—one of Mansfield's major brains, class president, *and* no tattoos."

Marine giggled. "How do you know, 'no tattoos'?"

"Oh ze French, ze French!" Imani answered back.

Vicky was preoccupied. She had a sudden mental image of taking Mark, or someone like Mark, home to meet her parents. Last week, she'd stayed behind after Maggie and Christie went in the dorm, and she'd talked to Teddy some more. She'd hoped to bring up her mother. After what Vicky had felt was almost ignoring her, Mrs. Lee had given her daughter a tight squeeze and kiss when she'd left, much to Vicky's surprise. But Teddy had problems of his own. He had been dating a

117

girl from Minnesota, not Chinese, not even Chinese-American, and his parents were having a hard time with it. They didn't forbid it—after all, Teddy was a man now—but they had made it clear that Caitlin wasn't really welcome at family functions. He and Vicky had discussed it for a long time. "I know it's complicated, saving face, plus a real fear on their part. We've suffered a great deal of prejudice in this country," Teddy had said. Now, Vicky wondered how her own parents would react. She'd never divided her friends into races, colors, or creeds. A friend was a friend. Had she learned this from her parents?

Maggie was talking about going home the following week during the Columbus Day break.

"I'm not homesick, but . . ." She didn't want to finish the sentence. What she wanted to say was, But I've never been away from my family on my birthday. She would be thirteen on October ninth. The trip home was one of her presents. Thirteen. Everybody else, it seemed, had been thirteen for so much longer. She wondered what this first year of her teens would bring. The year she had turned nine on the ninth, she'd been all excited and was certain it would be a special, lucky year. It had been her first year on Little Bittern, the first year of the inn, and it *was* an exciting time. As for this year, it had already been exciting enough.

"It's hard to believe she's only thirteen years old," Aleford's Chief of Police MacIsaac declared. *"I'd be proud to have someone like her on the force. The way she cracked this case would put any pro to shame! If you are agreeable, we'd like to consult you, Miss Porter, whenever we have a theft ring to break up. . . ."*

"Wake up, girl, we have to go back to work. We're

going home tomorrow and I have to finish a paper. I do not intend to do it this weekend. Our cousin is getting married and we plan to party seriously.''

After the guides left, the girls cleaned up and returned to room thirteen.

''We still aren't any further ahead than we were,'' Christie said.

Maggie was still caught up in her daydream, a daydream she wished desperately would come true. ''But nothing else has happened,'' she said.

''Not yet anyway.'' For once, Vicky was pessimistic.

❖Chapter Nine

"**D**ON'T WORRY, MY DAD WILL BE HERE any moment. You've got to get a move on or Maggie's going to miss her bus." Christie pushed her roommates out the front door of Widow and onto the porch. Friday's classes had ended early and the Cabot campus was emptying fast. Girls who weren't going home or to friends for the holiday weekend had moved to one dorm. There weren't too many of them.

Terry came flying out of her room, her face glowing. It wasn't hard to guess who was picking her up. Soon she was calling from the steps, "Art, Art, I'm all ready. Stay where you are."

The girls were a little disappointed. They hadn't had a chance to check out their housemother's boyfriend, Art Harrington, at close range. Maggie had had the best view so far. As Terry gathered her bags, including a teddy-bear knapsack, they tried to see as much as they could. He was driving Terry's car and had an impatient look on his handsome face.

"Are you going someplace nice?" Vicky asked

sweetly, to cover up her out-and-out nosiness. "It's supposed to be great weather this weekend."

"What? Oh, yes. I heard a weather report." Terry was either deliberately ignoring the question or, in her distracted state, hadn't taken it in. "I've got to go. You're all accounted for, right? Because I have to lock the dorm now."

"We're just leaving, but Christie's father hasn't come yet."

"He'll be here soon. Can't I wait inside? I promise I'll be sure the door's locked behind me."

Art gave a honk on the horn and Terry jumped a mile. "Okay, but if there's any problem, go over to Sudley House—that's where everyone is staying." She moved rapidly down the front walk.

"Bye, have fun," Maggie called, whispering to her friends, "Don't do anything we wouldn't do!"

"Right," said Vicky.

Terry waved from the car, jerking her hand in as Art screeched away from the dorm at top speed.

"Definitely not a parent-approved driver, and I was hoping for a ride to the bus. Come on, Maggie, we've got to run!" Vicky said. They hugged Christie goodbye, then told her to call Vicky if she got stuck. "There's plenty of room at the apartment and we'd have an excellent time." Then they were gone.

Christie walked back into the living room. The dorm was as silent as the grave. Those exact words came into her mind and she gave a little shudder. She'd been alone only two minutes and already she was having morbid thoughts. She went upstairs and checked on her supplies. She'd bought food, mostly the kind you could put in a mug and add hot water to, lots of granola bars, juice boxes, plus a bag of Oreo cookies she was going to try to eat without making crumbs. She might get terminally bored, but she wouldn't starve.

She sat down in the comfortable club chair that the Lees had donated to room thirteen and opened the book she was reading, Josephine Tey's *Brat Farrar*. She liked scary mysteries—and scary movies. All three roommates confessed to having seen *The Shining* at least four times. But she definitely didn't want to read anything remotely resembling Stephen King this weekend—when she'd be the sole occupant at Widow.

Cal Montgomery wasn't coming to pick her up. He didn't even know she had a break.

For once and for all, she was going to find out what was going on—and nobody was going to stop her.

"Did Christie seem a little out of it to you? Kind of nervous?" Maggie asked Vicky as they grabbed two seats in the back of the bus they'd caught by a few seconds. Once in Boston, Maggie would head for South Station and another bus. Vicky planned a stop at Filene's Basement, then home.

"Yeah, but I think it's probably hard for her to be in her house with just her father. It doesn't sound like she'd had anybody to really talk to about her mom's death, except maybe Hallie, the housekeeper. From the way she avoids the subject of her dad, I'd be surprised if she's been able to be open with him."

"Do you think we could convince her to go to the counseling service? For a start, she'd be able to get information about cancer and pregnancy. I know she's still thinking about it."

Vicky's face got stern. "Whenever I think about that

letter, I want to scream—and punch out whoever did it. Why don't we go to the counseling center and talk to someone? I know she'll be mad at first, but it's all superconfidential over there, and if we have some information, maybe we can persuade her to go."

"That's a good idea. That first night in our room, I knew she was dealing with something really heavy. You know that look she sometimes gets, sad and tired. I don't know how you could possibly ever get over losing your mother."

"You don't, but you can learn how to deal with it."

Vicky wondered how her own mother had dealt with the loss of not just her mother but also her father before she was Vicky's age. It had been in China, and afterward Virginia had been taken to Hong Kong to live with relatives she'd never met. Vicky heard the story from Teddy. Her mother never talked about her childhood. It was as if her life had only started when she met Mr. Lee.

On the bus bound north, Maggie got out the mystery she was reading, Mary Higgins Clark's latest, but despite the spell of the tale, Maggie was soon gazing out the window. The bright autumn landscape streaked past, already starting to fade in the late-afternoon shadows.

"The child has not spoken for three months, Doctor. You are the last hope. Appetite and sleep are normal, but since the mother died, not one word or sound."

"And of course nothing organic is wrong."

"There have been several examinations and the cause is purely psychological."

"Bring the child in and tell my secretary I am not to be disturbed on any account."

The group in the waiting room sat in hushed expecta-
tion. The doctor called out once for pizza. It was taken
as a good sign.

Three hours later, the door opened and Dr. Porter
motioned them in. The child was in her arms, sobbing,
"Mommy! I want my mommy! Where is she? Why can't
she come back?"

"A triumph," whispered one man. "A breakthrough
in the field. . . ."

The bus driver honked at a car passing on the right.
They'd crossed the border between New Hampshire and
Maine. Maggie would be home for dinner.

It was dark outside and Christie set her book aside
to get something to eat. She'd drawn the curtain in her
cubbyhole of a room and only turned on the light next
to her bed. She doubted anyone would notice, even the
security guards patrolling the campus. With so few people in residence, she imagined they'd be relaxing their
normal vigilance. At least she hoped so. The last thing
she wanted was to get caught before she could do the
catching.

The idea had come to her after the meet, after the
terrible letter. Her stomach still turned over when she
thought of it. The major thefts had occurred when the
dorm was asleep or empty, and what better time than
during a vacation? Marcia Lloyd was staying with one
of the day students right here in Aleford. She could
easily sneak back into Prentiss House. All she would
have had to do was leave her window unlocked. The
same reasoning applied to other Cabot—or Mansfield—
students. Stay at Sudley House or off campus, but
nearby, and leave a first-floor window open.

She felt a guilty pang when she thought about deceiving her roommates, but, she said to herself stubbornly, they might have tried to talk her out of it. The three of them couldn't very well have hidden in the dorm all weekend.

In any case, Christie was sure she had a long, long wait. It might not even be tonight, but tomorrow night. She took her flashlight and went into the common room, plugging in the electric kettle to heat some water for her soup. She settled into one of the chairs, keeping her eyes off the kettle. A watched pot never boils. But there was no hurry. She had all night.

For a while, she kept herself awake with her book, then with speculations. Mark Reese had discovered Christie's Sammy had been soaked in Lysol. That had been the smell, and if she had rubbed it all over her body, she would have felt itchy and uncomfortable for about twenty minutes, long enough to mess up her next dive and more than long enough to throw her off her concentration. Lysol was easy to get, of course. It made eliminating suspects difficult. But the person would have had to be able to get to her Sammy and would have to know a diver's routine. Marcia Lloyd's name leaped to mind—again.

By midnight, Christie was having trouble staying awake. She'd been up at six, as usual, to train before breakfast. She stood in the middle of her room and did twenty jumping jacks as fast as she could. It helped. It also helped warm her up. The heat was off, since the dorm was empty, and it was starting to get cold. She went to her closet to get a jacket.

Her closet was almost as big as the whole sleeping area. It had been left untouched when the original house was remodeled and she had graciously donated some of its space to Vicky. She pulled the string on the lightbulb that was suspended in the center. It was warm and cozy. If it got too cold in the other room, she could always sleep in here. She put on her jacket and reached for the cord to turn the light off. She looked up at the fixture. Next to it, she could detect the faint outlines of a large square. She'd never really noticed it before, not having had occasion to stand in her closet for any length of time.

She went into her room and got the chair from her desk. Standing on it, she was able to push against the ceiling, and sure enough, the square gave way. It was a trapdoor! Dust fell and, even more disgusting, a shower of dead flies.

"Ugh!" Christie said out loud, and jumped off the chair.

Suddenly, she realized where the opening led. Dead flies and dust. The cupola, the widow's walk. They had assumed it must be above their room; they just hadn't figured how close!

She decided to go to the bathroom to wash her hands. She closed the closet door, leaving the chair still in place. She'd clean it up tomorrow.

It was halfway down the hall that she first heard voices. Terrified, she stopped to listen.

They were on the floor below!

Christie's heart began to beat faster. Confronting them was a dangerous idea. What else? Going back to her room and waiting for them to find her wasn't much better. Should she try to hide, or get away and call the police? She had really only planned on proving her theory. She hadn't actually thought ahead to what she'd do if intruders did in fact break in. She turned around and tiptoed silently back to room thirteen. She needed to think.

They were not allowed to have phones in their rooms, a situation Vicky bewailed often. There were two pay phones in big, old-fashioned wooden booths on the first floor. Privacy—once you got a turn. She could try to slip down, but Christie had no idea where the thieves were, and the thought of walking straight into two or more criminals busily looting what they thought was an empty dorm sent shivers up her spine. She opened her door and poked her head out into the darkness. A man's voice shouted, "Hurry up! I'm going to the third floor. We've got to be on the road soon if we're going to meet Chet at Alewife. I don't want to be driving around with all this stuff any longer than I have to."

It wasn't a Cabot student!

Christie closed her door, allowed herself one second to panic, then raced into her closet. Up into the widow's walk with the fly cadavers. It was her only chance! Even if they did open her closet door, she'd be able to get onto the roof and away before they found her.

She stood on the chair, pushed the trapdoor to one side, and hoisted herself up, keeping her mouth tightly closed. It was a good thing she was in shape, and it was unlikely they could follow her—unless they'd explored Widow enough to know about the attic.

It had been a man's voice. But not Mr. Pritchard's. They'd been wrong about him—and Marcia. But who was it? She wracked her brains but couldn't place it.

She carefully replaced the square of wood. She'd turned off the closet light and had her flashlight tucked in her waistband.

Standing up in the glassed-in cupola, she looked out across the campus. The moon had risen, but it wasn't giving much light—only a slim Cheshire cat smile. She allowed herself to smile, as well. She was safe—for now. All she had to do was get down from the roof and call the police.

She opened the door and walked out onto the flat roof. How had the raccoon done it? Christie peered over one side. There was a drainpipe, but while it may have held an extremely large raccoon, she didn't trust it to hold her. The lights along the pathways were on and there were several bright lights by Widow's garage and at the front of the house, as well. She paced around the edge of the roof, but there was no way down, unless it really was Wonderland and she suddenly sprouted wings, flying to her own turret below, then scrambling down the shingles.

Without the voices, her courage returned—and her anger. Why had these strangers sent those notes and deliberately made everyone suspicious of her? She had to get to a phone! And the nearest one she knew of was downstairs.

There was only one thing to do.

They had never gotten around to telling Terry about the broken window in the attic. Christie easily removed the louvers and crept in. Now all you have to do is get down the stairs and phone. No sweat, she told herself bravely. Suddenly, she thrust her hand into her pocket in alarm. Did she have any change? She let her breath out in relief. She did. She also had Teddy's number and remembered she'd been wearing the same jacket that night in Brookline. Would the police believe her story?

Or maybe she should call Teddy first and get him to call the police?

She opened the attic door. It creaked and she froze. The voices were on the third floor now. It was a good thing she hadn't tried to get to the stairs by going down the hallway. Getting to them by way of the roof was certainly roundabout, but it had worked—so far.

From the sound of it, they were at the end of the floor, at the opposite side of the house. Christie started down the stairs. She had to hope they hadn't left a lookout elsewhere in the dorm. She slipped down past the third floor and kept going, looking back over her shoulder quickly to make sure she wasn't being followed.

The stairs were dark and she had to concentrate on not falling. She was on the second floor. She stopped. No one was coming. Total silence.

The first floor. She went straight to the phone booth. Time was of the essence and she decided to call the police.

Chief Charley MacIsaac was on the night shift. This wasn't all that unusual. He'd never been one for special privileges, and Officer O'Donnell had a new baby at home. Uninterrupted slumber was getting to be a rarity in O'Donnell's life and Chief MacIsaac had volunteered to take over the shift.

The phone seldom rang past nine o'clock much of anywhere in Aleford, and Chief MacIsaac was dozing himself when the strident ring sent his chair crashing to the floor. He picked himself up, unhurt but annoyed, and grabbed the receiver.

"There are burglars at Prentiss House at the Cabot School," a female voice whispered.

"What? I can't hear you. You'll have to talk louder."

"I can't. I'm in the phone booth on the first floor and they're upstairs. This is not a joke. Someone named Chet is waiting for the stolen goods at Alewife. Call Teddy. The number is five-five-five–seven-eight-nine-zero. He's my friend's cousin. Tell him Christie called you. He can—"

The phone went dead. Chief MacIsaac scratched his head. Kids. Now what the devil was this all about?

Christie looked up from where she'd crouched down in the booth to make the call.

"Well, well, what have we here? That had better have been your boyfriend you were talking to, missy. Nobody likes a stool pigeon."

She hadn't known the voice, but she knew the face that was leering sinisterly in the beam of his flashlight.

Art Harrington.

And Terry, their housemother, was right behind him.

❖Chapter Ten

"WHAT IN THE WORLD ARE YOU DOING here? You're supposed to be home!" Terry gasped.

"What are *you* doing here!" Christie stood up. She couldn't believe it, her own housemother! "How could you do this to us? You let everyone think we were stealing things, when all along it was you who was ripping us off! And sending me those letters!" Christie was close to tears in her rage.

"Letters? I never sent you any letters, and I didn't know people thought you were responsible for the thefts. You should have told me." Oddly enough, Terry's voice held a note of concern.

"I hate to break up this tender moment, babe, but we have to get going. Think you can carry the TV to the car while I take care of her?"

The TV! Christie had a wildly inappropriate thought. Maggie was going to be really ticked off at missing *Friends,* her favorite show. Then Art's final words sunk in—"take care of her." How?

The same thought occurred to Terry. "You're not going to hurt her, are you?" she asked anxiously.

"Not if she cooperates, starting with telling me who she just called." Art's eyes bored into Christie's. How could she ever have thought him handsome? At the moment, he looked disgusting. She began to feel sick with fear.

"You were right. It was Teddy, my boyfriend," she lied, stammering slightly for real. "He was supposed to meet me here."

Art smiled, a very mean smile. "Not one of those little goody-goodies, are you?"

Terry looked shocked. "You were going to be here alone with a boy? You know that's against the rules."

Christie thought Terry was in no position to be preaching about rules—when here she was with a trunkful of stolen property. Where were the police? Did Chief MacIsaac think the call was a prank?

"I knew it was wrong. I'm sorry," she said, trying to keep the conversation going and stall for time.

"Look, forget the TV. I'll get it when we leave. Just find me some rope. Maybe it's true about her boyfriend. Maybe not, but I don't want to take any chances of having someone on our trail too soon. I just want to put her on ice for the weekend. Nothing major."

"The weekend!" Christie was really frightened now. Tied up and locked in. What if no one found her! "You can't do that—"

Art had reached the end of his patience. "Shut up! I've had enough. . . ." He reached out to slap Christie across the face, but Terry screamed and jumped in the way, taking the blow instead.

"Now look what you made me do! You are really dumb! Get the rope and get it fast."

Terry was rubbing the ugly red mark his hand had

132

made on her face. "No—no, I don't think so," she said slowly.

Christie wanted to cheer, but she kept her mouth closed, her eyes wide with fear for herself—and now for Terry, too.

"What are you talking about?"

"It was one thing, looking the other way while you took stuff, even though I knew it wasn't right"— she looked apologetically at Christie—"but this is different."

"She's a rich brat like all the rest of them. Their mommies and daddies will just buy them more. And nobody's going to hurt her. We have to keep her from squealing until we're long gone."

Terry shook her head. "I can't let you do this. She could suffocate or something."

Art looked at her. "Fine, babe. Then it's going to be both of you. No big deal. Now start walking. You two can tell each other your life stories in that closet in your room, Ms. Housemother. The locked one."

Terry had been keeping valuables in a large storage closet in her suite. Christie was pretty sure it was as bare as Mother Hubbard's cupboard about now.

"Get going," Art snarled, motioning for them to go ahead of him down the hall. He gave Christie a poke in the back—a hard poke.

Christie went. She glanced back at Terry. It was hard to read the expression on her face—fear, sadness, and something else—could it be relief?

Art was extremely ticked off, Christie couldn't help but notice. He started muttering angrily, cataloging all Terry's shortcomings. Then his voice got louder and more menacing. "I should have known what a wuss you'd turn out to be when you made me bring that bracelet back! I could have gotten more than a buck or two for it. If the kid is stupid enough to leave it lying around . . .'' He stopped after a few well-chosen curses and told them to hurry up. Christie could feel her own fear reflecting off Terry.

Inside the housemother's suite, Art opened the closet door, and Christie knew that if she was going to do anything, she had to do it now—and fast.

"Grab him, Terry," she screamed, tackling Art's legs. He fell facedown and Terry sat on his back. The attack took Art totally by surprise, as Christie had hoped. Before he could collect what little wits he had, Christie instructed Terry, "Shove him in the closet!" The two pushed his still-prone body with all their strength and slammed the door tightly. Terry turned the key in the lock. Almost immediately, they heard the sound of Art's fists hammering on the back of the door. The other, more welcome sound they heard was the siren of a police car.

"I'm sorry, Christie. I've been a total jerk. I thought he was the sun and the moon. Nobody's ever cared for me the way he said he did."

Christie comforted her housemother. "Love makes people do some very crazy things." Or so I've been told, she added silently.

They ran down the hall to let the police in the front door and quickly told them what had happened. Terry took full responsibility for her part. It was impossible for Christie to keep back her tears as Terry was read her rights.

"I thought you wouldn't believe me," Christie said

to the police chief after Terry had been taken away. They were sitting in the living room and could hear Art once again swearing his head off at the police, Christie, Terry, and the world in general as he, too, was arrested. Christie felt a chill of fear, even with Aleford's finest so close.

"We take every call seriously and you *can* believe me, but I think you have some things to set straight. For starters, what were you doing here in the dorm all by yourself?"

Before Christie could explain—and she had a feeling it was not an explanation he was going to be real happy with—his beeper went off.

"Got to get this," he said, and went out to the car, returning after a few minutes with a big smile on his face.

"The Cambridge police picked up this guy Chet. Turns out he's an old friend of theirs and they've been looking for him in connection with a series of house breaks. We'll get warrants to search his place and this Art fellow's. I wouldn't be surprised if Christmas comes early this year for a lot of folks who thought they'd never see their stuff again. According to the Cambridge guys, Chet likes to sit on things for a while until they cool off a little."

Maybe Marcia would get her CD player back after all. Christie hoped so. After all, Miss Lloyd had been their prime suspect. A little voice nagged at Christie: But what about the letters? Terry had seemed genuinely puzzled when Christie mentioned them. The case wasn't closed yet.

The door to the room burst open just as MacIsaac

was asking Christie how to get in touch with her father. Vicky came running in, followed by Teddy.

"Did I miss everything! Why didn't you call me? You could have gotten yourself killed!" Vicky blurted out.

"So, you called Teddy." Christie faced Chief Mac-Isaac. "I thought you believed me."

"I did, but on the way here, I had the dispatcher get in touch with this young man, who turned out to be a bit hard to find. We try to get all the information we can."

"I was at the Ginger Jar with my family. The police reached my roommate, who fortunately knew where I was."

"And there was no way I was staying home." Vicky was adamant.

It had taken a few minutes to convince the Lees that Teddy would keep a very close eye on his cousin. Arriving at Cabot's front entrance, they passed a police car leaving the scene, which convinced Teddy that it was safe to proceed and Vicky that she had missed the best part.

"Tell me everything. You didn't go home because you thought the burglar would try again when the dorm was empty. Good thinking, but definitely no repeats. Christie and Company does not go in for solos. So who was it?" Vicky was still so excited that she was moving from subject to subject like a pinball machine.

"You're never going to believe this. It was Terry, and her boyfriend, Art!"

For an instant, Vicky was actually speechless; then the dam burst again. "What is this dorm—jinxed or something? Last year, they had the runaway bride and this year we have Bonnie and Clyde?''

Christie spoke to Chief MacIsaac, who had settled back comfortably in one of the wing chairs, enjoying the scene. ''I know what she did was breaking the law and majorly wrong, but Terry is not a bad person. The guy kind of hypnotized her, like in this weird old movie I saw—*Svengali.* And she did protect me in the end.''

''All this will be taken into consideration, but being easily influenced is no excuse for harming others. When you're an adult, you have to take full responsibility for your own actions. You're learning that now. For instance, even though you did catch a pair of crooks, you weren't supposed to be here this weekend, were you? Bet you told quite a few whoppers, too.''

Christie flushed. ''Well, yes, but—''

''No 'buts.' '' The chief was firm.

''Okay,'' Christie whispered.

She had to explain the whole thing again when Mrs. Babcox appeared, obviously roused from her bed, her hair still covered by a net. The living room was beginning to get pretty crowded and it was taking on a slightly festive air. Teddy and Vicky had made coffee and cocoa. They were all consuming Christie's bag of Oreos.

''I really thought she had grown up. I've known Theresa since she was a child. Scatterbrained yes, and a follower, not a leader, but in the last few years she'd pulled her life together and was doing well at school. I'll never be able to forgive myself for misjudging the situation so drastically.'' Mrs. Babcox was envisioning the phone ringing off the hook from one parent after another. She took another Oreo. "Thank God no one was hurt. And of course the school will prosecute," she told Chief MacIsaac.

He nodded. "Think you might feel better after a chat with Christie here. The housemother refused to go along with her boyfriend at the end. When we arrived, he was fit to be tied, locked in the storage closet by the two young women."

"Is this true?"

"Yes," Christie said. "I don't think Terry realized how bad her boyfriend was until he threatened someone. He had given her this big line about all of us being so rich, we wouldn't miss the things they took."

Vicky sneered. " 'Boy fiend' is more like it. Some women have terrible taste in men."

"And what do you know about it, little cousin? I have to get you home or Aunt Virginia and Uncle Henry, not to mention Grandmother, will decide *I'm* a fiend."

"Why doesn't Christie come home with me?" Vicky suggested. "She can't stay here, and they haven't made any arrangements for her to stay at the other dorm."

Christie liked the idea. She wanted to get a little distance from her night at Widow for a day or two. "My father is out of town, and you can check to make sure. I really didn't tell too many lies."

The Lees were called and arrangements made. Mrs. Babcox was relieved to have Christie looked after over the holiday. The full impact might not have hit yet.

The girl could have been seriously injured—or worse.

The eighth grade returned and found yet another housemother in residence—Mrs. Babcox's widowed sister-in-law. In defiance of any stereotypes, the other

Mrs. Babcox, as she came to be known, was an athletic woman in her early sixties who was still working part-time for the Aleford School Department. "Call me Babbie," she told the girls Monday night after gathering them together for a meeting—during which, the events of the weekend were related once more for the two or three students who had somehow been missed as the news traveled around the campus at roughly the speed of light.

After the meeting, the three roommates were sitting with their guides in the third-floor common room when an interesting delegation appeared at the door. It was headed by Marcia. Her clique and a few other eighth graders trailed behind.

"I want to apologize for some of the suspicion that has been directed your way," Marcia said bravely.

"You notice she doesn't say 'all,'" Imani whispered to Maggie, who jabbed her in the side. This was no time to start laughing. Marcia was looking superintense.

There was a pause while the class president waited for one of the girls to say that it was all right, accepting the apology. Except no one spoke.

"I mean, it wasn't fair suspecting you," Ellie said. "It was just because we didn't know you."

This time, Vicky did speak up. "That's the whole thing. You didn't know us, so we became immediate targets. You didn't take the time to talk to us. It's like judging someone by the color of his or her skin, or religion, or nationality."

"Maybe we can learn from this," Aisha said. "There are going to be a lot of new girls next year."

Marcia took the lead, of course. "You're right. It wasn't fair—and it won't happen again."

"The letters were the worst part. You don't have to admit who sent them. Just never, never do it to anyone else again." Christie's voice trembled with emotion, but she said what she had wanted to say.

"What letters?" It was like Terry all over again. The girls looked at one another, bewildered. "Who were they sent to and what did they say?" Tina wanted to know.

"Never mind. It's not important now, and I have a feeling there won't be any more."

After a few last words, everyone said good night and the girls from room thirteen went wearily off to bed. Tomorrow meant classes again, and very little homework had been done over the long weekend.

Maggie was the first to bring up the subject of the letters. They were just about to turn out the lights.

"You had your turn, Christie—and by the way, in the future I think we should make a promise to keep each other informed. There is that part about 'and Company.'"

"I know, I know. Vicky's already yelled at me, too, but I thought it was the right move."

"Anyway. It's our turn now. Vicky and I will unmask the poison-pen author, who is the same person who soaked your Sammy in Lysol, or my name is not Margaret Porter."

"Wow, look at what being one year older has done," Christie teased. "But be my guest."

"I assume you'll tell me all about this in the morning, Margaret dear," Vicky said, yawning.

"Of course, Victoria, and if you think about it a bit, you'll figure it out, too."

"I probably have."

*　　*　　*

Sixth graders were not allowed to board, but they had space in the main classroom building as a kind of lounge and place to do homework. Late Tuesday afternoon, Maggie and Vicky walked in and sat down on a couch behind the door.

"Nice place. That poster of Keanu Reeves next to the 'Hang in there, Kitty' one is tasteful, don't you think?" Vicky looked around the room, amused at the sixth graders' choices.

"Definitely," Maggie agreed. She was wearing the present Willy had given her for her birthday—a blood-splattered sweatshirt, complete with dagger and a public-television *Mystery* series logo. It seemed particularly appropriate. "You remember your part, right?" she added.

"I thought I was the actress. Of course I remember," Vicky protested. The two had settled on a "good cop/bad cop" routine for what they intended to do. The problem was, they were so angry that they both wanted to be the "bad cop." They flipped a coin and Maggie won.

The door opened and several sixth graders walked in, loudly complaining about a social studies test they'd just had. Vicky gave Maggie a wink. Their quarry was one of the group.

Maggie stood up. "If you don't mind, we have something we'd like to discuss with Jessica here in private." Whether it was her tone of voice or the fact that she was an eighth grader, the girls quickly left, darting questioning looks over their shoulders at Jessie. Maggie shut the door firmly behind them.

"What's going on? What do you want with me?" Jessica asked in a slightly belligerent tone. She looked like a smaller version of her sister, except her hair was cut short for diving, an indication of how seriously she took her sport—even more seriously than her sister did.

Maggie got straight to the point. "We know what you did. We want to know why and how you're going to make up for it."

Jessie looked scared. "I—"

Vicky interrupted. "Look, why don't we sit down and talk this over together calmly." Jessie gave her, the "good cop," a grateful look.

They sat down. Jessica took a deep breath but didn't say anything. Apparently, she had decided that silence in her case would be golden. It was Maggie's turn again.

"We have all day, all night. And we don't intend to leave your side until you admit that you sent those horrible letters to Christie and tried to get her to mess up at the meet. Believe me, we have proof."

At the mention of proof, Jessica's face clouded. "You're not being fair! Just because I'm younger, you think—"

Again, Vicky interrupted. "Do you think it was fair to try to make someone do badly in a sports events and accuse her of things she never did? Put yourself in her place. How would you feel?" Vicky's words were harsh, but her tone was gentle and slightly sad. "And the one about her mother . . ." Vicky let her voice trail off. It really had been a horrible thing to do.

The technique was working. "I never meant to hurt her." Jessie was getting weepy.

"Then why did you do it?" Maggie delivered the knockout punch.

"At first, it was just to give her a hard time, because she was new. Everybody was doing it, my sister and all her friends. Then she turned up on the swim team. She was making Marcia look bad!''

"Maybe she was making you look a little less than perfect, too,'' Maggie suggested.

Jessie was crying for real. "Okay, maybe I was jealous. I guess I'd gotten used to being the star after last year. I never thought I'd be better at anything than Marcia. But then Christie had to come along. I really hated her!''

Maggie forced herself to remember that last letter. She didn't want to start feeling sorry for Jessie.

"Here's the deal. You've got to go to Mrs. Babcox and Coach Stevens and tell them the whole thing or we will. We'll give you the chance to confess, and maybe the fact that you've come forward yourself will help. But if we find out you haven't, then we'll do it ourselves. And you have to tell your sister and her friends.''

"Maybe you should tell them and your parents first. They might go with you when you see the coach and the headmistress,'' Vicky advised. "You really need some help to deal with how you felt and what you did.''

"My parents!'' Jessie's voice was bitter. "My father and his new family live in California. Marcia and I get a card with some money in it on our birthdays and at Christmas. And my mother lives in Switzerland. That's where her friends are, she says. At least we see her in the summer.''

"Then where do you live?'' Vicky asked.

"I board with the family of another sixth grader in Aleford. They're really more like my own family, except for Marcia.''

Now Maggie did feel sorry for her, but, wanting to

143

bring things to a close, she said, "So what are you going to do?"

"Walk back to Widow with you, if you'll let me, and talk to Marcia. Then go see Mrs. Babcox. I only hope she doesn't kick me out of school."

Which you deserve, Maggie said to herself, but I hope she doesn't, either.

Jessica Lloyd didn't get expelled, but she lost every privilege a sixth grader has and the coach barred her from competition for the season, although she would still be allowed to train. Jessica, much to everyone's surprise, did stay on the team, training hard. She even began to ask Christie for help on some of her dives.

"I don't know how you figured it out," Christie said to her roommates. Once again, they were drinking cocoa that Maggie had made. It was the night before another meet.

"Elementary—we just eliminated all the other suspects," Maggie answered with a broad smile. "Marcia and her friends really didn't seem to have a clue about the letters. It's hard for everyone to fake surprise like that at the same time. Plus, the person who sent the letters had to be the same one lousing you up at the meet. Someone who knew where your locker was and someone who was in and out of Widow. She was able to put the first letter in your mailbox while we were at the Cape. Anyone seeing her here would have just assumed she was getting something from her sister's room."

"She does deny tripping you, so that's still up in the air," Vicky added. "Although she admitted she had a friend drop a book when you were doing your last dive and she did tamper with your Sammy." Vicky was slightly chagrined that Maggie had figured out it was Jessie before she had, but then she reminded herself that she hadn't read even half the mysteries Maggie had.

"Someone did trip me," Christie asserted. "But at the time, I had so many enemies, it could have been anybody." While not exactly becoming Miss Cabot, as she had told her father the night before school started—could it only have been a month ago?—she and her roommates were now encountering smiles and offers to sit with groups at meals.

"Oh!" Vicky put her hand to her mouth. "I can't believe I almost forgot to tell you! I meant to right away!"

"Tell us what? I mean, tell us," Maggie implored.

Vicky started to giggle. "Mr. Pritchard! I found out about Mr. Pritchard!"

The girls had been making discreet inquiries, but no one seemed to know anything about his private life.

Imani, who had him for English, said, "Honey, believe me, that man has no private life."

Vicky continued. "At our rehearsal today, the two of them walked in together and sat in the back row. I was sure I would totally blow my lines, but I didn't, and they stayed through the whole thing. At the end, the director introduced them to everyone. She's his *daughter* and studying theater at Emerson College in Boston. Next term, she's going to work with the club on a series of plays written by students in some course she's taking. They're all about what it's like to be a teenager."

"What was she wearing?" Christie was surprised Vicky hadn't started with a description of the young woman's outfit.

"Kind of the same type of dress, silk, but blue, and she had a really neat embroidered vest over it. The guys from Mansfield were acting like total morons, asking her these 'serious' questions while they were drooling all over her."

Christie yawned. "I'm sorry to be such a party pooper, but I have to get up at the crack of dawn tomorrow—the meet's not at home, remember—so I'll say good night. Anyway, it looks like all the mysteries have been solved."

She left them and went to bed. Vicky and Maggie didn't stay up much later. They crept quietly into the room. Soon, Maggie heard Vicky's soft, regular breathing, but Maggie herself was wide awake.

Christie and Company had really worked. They had accomplished what they had set out to do and she knew she had made two friends for life. She tried to picture them all grown up, careers, marriage.... It was hard, even for someone with her imagination. Marriage—that was a tough one to think about. At least Christie had Scott obviously interested in her and Vicky's crush on Mark would no doubt lead to others. Maggie had had boys who were friends, but she'd always felt shy at the idea of being with someone in particular.

"How is it that I've never seen you before? You say you've been at Cabot since eighth grade? At least we'll have senior year and then, who knows, Maggie? It was your poem, of course. The one in the literary magazine. I knew I had to meet the person who wrote it or die disappointed...."

Maggie's head jerked. Was she asleep or awake? Asleep.

*   *   *

146

The meet was half over. Christie was doing very well and so was Marcia. At the last practice, she had actually admitted to Christie that having her on the team was making Marcia work harder. "I guess I like competition," she said. When Christie reported the conversation back to her roommates, Vicky had declared, "Good, because she's not going to be the only one running for class president next year."

But Marcia had never said anything to Christie about what Jessie had done, although the coach had talked with the whole team about it, much to Christie's embarrassment. The two sisters were closer than ever, Christie noticed, and she hoped Jessie was getting some help. Sometimes people needed a good counselor, not someone they saw in their everyday lives. Someone they could say anything to—and not have to see over breakfast.

She was surprised at the thought and wondered where it had come from. Vicky had been saying something similar in regard to Jessie. Maggie had been talking about how good the counseling center at Cabot was supposed to be, too. Christie wondered . . .

The bus trip to the other school had been great. Scott had instantly claimed the place next to Christie. "You're not one of those people who has to have total silence before competing, are you?" he'd asked. "No way," she'd answered, and the trip had flown by. They'd separated to change and wished each other luck. Mansfield was doing as well as Cabot, and Christie had watched with pride as Scott led his team during the first round.

As was to be expected, most of the onlookers were from the other school. Suddenly, one of Christie's teammates nudged her. "Aren't those some of your friends?" Christie looked up into the bleachers. Maggie and Vicky were making their way to places at the top, where they'd have a good view. How on earth did they get here? Christie wondered, thrilled that they'd bothered to come. Teddy? There was someone following behind them.

She got a huge lump in her throat as a familiar figure began to wave in her direction, a big smile on his face.

It wasn't Teddy. It was her father.

Cal Montgomery raised his long arms up over his head, hands clasped together, and shook them in her direction. Christie went up to do her next dive, but first she returned his salute.

She stood and trained her eyes at the end of the board.

''This one's for you, Dad—and you, Mom,'' she whispered. Then she flew through the air.